Praise for OILY:

"Angus Woodward has invented a sly and funny new literary form all his own: the novel as a 'Terms of Use' agreement. Add space aliens, oil spills, and a touchingly effective modern-day love story, and you'll get some idea of what he's up to in OILY. Highly recommended for fans of Vonnegut, Warner Bros., and anyone who's ever wondered what's really included in those user contracts."

- George Bishop, author of THE NIGHT OF THE COMET

"In his lustrous and highly lubricated novel, OILY, Angus Woodward has come unstuck in time, sure, but also within the matrix of the whole carbon-chain construct of narrative convention. Lathering layers upon layers of healthy meta-fictions and hearty surrealities, he creates a piquant parquet of polyunsaturated satiric strata. Good for him! Good for us all! While deploying a host of alienating effects (and aliens to boot) OILY discombobulates us, a bath of defamiliarization, all surplus, the world stripped down to its pieces, reassembled into something strange but utilitarian like a Jeep, reduced to all its parts, packed in Cosmoline, made ready to hit the road.

- Michael Martone author of BROODING and THE MOON OVER WAPAKONETA

Angus Woodward's OILY is more than slightly hallucinatory, very inventive meta-science fiction. What's not to like? Take your pick— Its endless funny soliloquies, its charmingly askew descriptions, its many layered tale or its exceptionally astute, petite aliens— I don't want to spoil it for you—-try it for yourself. Enjoy.

- Moira Crone author of, among several other books, THE NOT YET, finalist for the Philip K. Dick Award, 2012

OILY

Angus Woodward

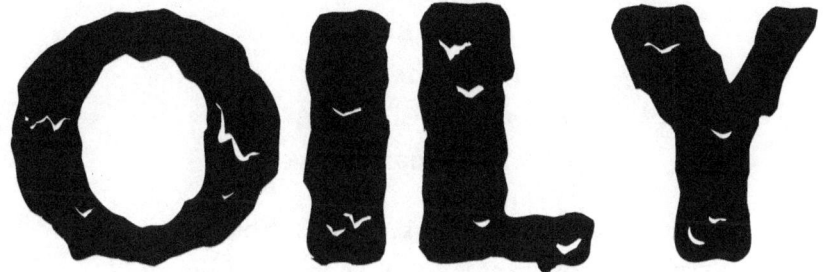

OILY

Angus Woodward

SPACEBOY BOOKS

Denver, Colorado

Published in the United States by:
Spaceboy Books LLC
1627 Vine Street
Denver, CO 80206
www.readspaceboy.com

First printed October 2018

ISBN: 978-0-9997862-4-6

This book is dedicated to the memory of those injured and killed by the British Petroleum/Transocean fiasco.

Oily
TERMS OF USE

BY CLICKING "I AGREE" BELOW, YOU ACCEPT THE TERMS OF THIS AGREEMENT REGARDING THE USE, RE-USE, ABUSE, AND NON-USE OF THIS PRODUCT ("PRODUCT") HENCEFORTH AND FOREVER, REGARDLESS OF NATURAL DISASTER; CHANGES TO INTERNATIONAL, FEDERAL, STATE, AND LOCAL ORDINANCES; SPILLS OF TOXIC AND NON-TOXIC SUBSTANCES; THE END OF LITERATURE AS A VIABLE ART FORM; AND ANY OTHER FORESEEN OR UNFORESEEN EVENT OR PHENOMENON COVERED OR NOT COVERED BY ALL EXPRESS OR IMPLICIT WARRANTIES.

I. ACCEPTANCE OF TERMS

Oily: A Novel ("Oily") welcomes you. Oily provides you with the services described below and herein according to the terms of this agreement, which may be updated from time to time without notice to you. By accessing and using Oily's services, you accept and agree to be bound by the terms and provisions of the Terms of Use (TOU). In addition, when discussing the content of Oily with others (including but not limited to friends, acquaintances, co-workers, family members, and healthcare professionals), you agree to abide by certain articles of the agreement and to represent the contents of Oily with an acceptable degree of accuracy, fairness, and perspicacity, even if you do not know the meaning of "perspicacity."

II. DESCRIPTION OF SERVICES

Oily provides users with an account of fictional events experienced and/or carried out by fictional characters. Any resemblance, factual or perceived, between past, present, or future persons or events is strictly coincidental or the result of author clairvoyance, for which the creator of Oily shall not be held responsible by any person, place, or thing. You understand that certain resemblances between characters and events within this product and persons and events in the real world ("reality") are inevitable and by no means evidence of fraud, slander, or malice of any kind. As an example, Oily begins with a character named Warren, a resident of New Orleans, Louisiana ("NOLA") unlocking the side door of a small house and pushing into the house "with such energy that the door didn't stick and creak the way it always did on steamy spring days." The fictional character Warren ("Warren") subsequently shouts "Penny," at the same time "betting that she is awake by now," then further shouting, "You've got to see this." The product further states that by the time Warren gets to the bedroom, Penny is raising herself up off the pillow, wincing a bit as she moves. "What's wrong?" she asks, the sand in her voice telling Warren that she had still been asleep. Warren subsequently makes an effort to slow himself down, taking a deep breath as he sits on the end of the bed, facing her. "I found this thing. This weird thing," he tells her, and she says, "Okay," both of them knowing (after a decade of marriage) that "okay" in this context means *okay that's not the first time you've said "I found this thing" or its equivalent in the past year or so, ever since I got sick and you started taking almost daily walks along the canal at the edge of our neighborhood. I was sort of interested in the feathers and the desiccated crab shell, but I was repulsed by the long orange nutria teeth you pulled from a rotting skull. As your loving wife, I will listen with an open mind, even though I'm not feeling particularly good this morning and for once I was sleeping past eight, because if I did feel good I would be interested and I would be out there with you ogling birds and watching fish jump. So let's take a minute and look at whatever it is, and then move on to my morning meds and some strong ginger tea.* Whereupon Warren nods, slowed further by the weight of Penny's "Okay." The edges of his hair are sweaty. "I sat down in the grass by this one little willow that grows right by the water. I stop there a lot. Sometimes I see garfish hanging out in the shadows of the willow, and it's just a fairly peaceful spot," he begins, and Penny says, "Uh-huh," meaning *Just show me whatever you found and let's move on.* Warren grimaces apologetically (and Penny accepts his apology with a blink) and begins to describe a sound he heard, "kind of like the sound of a jet passing overhead, except quiet and only lasting a sec. Anyway, then I looked down and found this." He holds out his hand. A matte black object lies across his palm. Penny shrugs. "Looks like a fat pen or something. Could you maybe—."

"Feel it," Warren says.

"Is it clean?"

"It was just lying in the grass next to me, after I heard that sound." He extends his hand further, and Penny obliges, probably figuring doing so might get her closer to morning meds and ginger tea. The object feels warm and exceedingly smooth. Unlike a pen, it is seamless, pointless, and clipless. Its ends are blunt, one with a little nib. A faint textured circle covers the nibless end.

"Is it plastic or metal?" she asks.

"I can't tell," Warren says. "At first I thought it might be some kind of stylus, maybe for the latest video game or whatever. For about a minute I thought it came off a tree."

"It looks like an acorn."

"Exactly! Like a long, black acorn with no cap."

"Wow," Penny says, and hands the object back to Warren. She does her best to smile, glancing at the grove of medicine bottles on the bedside table, eyebrows raised helpfully.

Warren stands, pushing the black acorn into his jeans pocket. He starts opening bottles, shaking out pills and lining them up beside Penny's water glass. Two round white ones, a lavender one, a pink one, and an oblong white one. Penny hands him the near-empty glass, like always. He nods and stands up straight but hesitates before heading to the kitchen to refill the glass and start the ginger tea. Penny looks up at him and tilts her head. "One more thing," he says quietly.

"What?"

"The acorn thing? I saw it fly."

Penny cocks her head, widens her eyes. "Warren?" she calls, but he is already halfway to the kitchen.

THE ABOVE PRODUCT EXCERPT AND ALL OTHER PRODUCT EXCERPTS ARE OFFERED FOR DEMONSTRATION PURPOSES ONLY AND ARE PROTECTED BY COPYRIGHT.

Should you happen to know or be a person named Warren or Penny and/or know or be a resident of NOLA and/or reside in a small house with a door that sticks on humid days, and/or be or know any person or circumstances or events similar to those depicted above or elsewhere in the product, you understand that such occurrences are mere coincidences, in no way indicating espionage or conspiracy by the creator of Oily. Furthermore, as user of Oily you understand that there is no point in reading too much into the fact that the creator of Oily is also named Warren, refraining, for example, from assuming that the creator of Oily has a wife named Penny (even if he does) or a small house with a door that sticks on steamy spring days. Kindly refrain from assuming that the creator of Oily believes that alien life forms capable of interstellar travel played a role in the 2010 catastrophe known colloquially as "the BP™ oil spill."

III. USER QUALIFICATIONS

By reading and continuing to read Oily, whether you have procured the product from the creator's website, received it as a gift, borrowed it from any person or institution, or found it years from now on an old hard drive retrieved from the dumpster of a nearby office building, you agree that you meet certain conditions as stated below:

A. Reading ability and experience

You possess the ability to read documents of considerable length, with or without drawings, photographs, pictures, depictions, or illustrations of any kind; with or without chapters, paragraphs, sentences, and other parts of considerable length and/or brevity. Your vocabulary is such that words including but not limited to "transmogrify," "planetary," "surreptitiously," and "bung" will cause little if any confusion, and you hold Oily blameless for such confusion as does occur and instead blame your own shortcomings and/or the educational system and/or today's high-tech fast-paced short-attention-span lifestyle.

Furthermore, you possess a familiarity with the conventions of written communication, particularly novels, such that abrupt shifts in point of view fail to bewilder you. By clicking "Agree" below, you confirm that you have read the TOU and agree to hold Oily and its creator blameless in the event of disorientation caused by abrupt shifts in point of view, and you affirm that the creator of Oily has alerted you to the frequency of abrupt shifts from the points of view of human, earthbound characters (which are fictional) to the points of view of fictional alien characters such as Jerry, who a few hours before Warren's conversation with Penny (see Article II) descended to the cargo bay of a smooth black spaceship held in geosynchronous orbit 188 miles above Warren and Penny's little wood-frame house.

Before proceeding, you are instructed to read the following product sample:

Jerry pauses in front of the cargo bay viewport, doing his best to ignore his companion for the morning, an intern named Phthsspitty-snapp. The little blue, white and green planet below looks promising, the colors of its oceans and continents signaling the presence of bountiful life.

Phthsspitty-snapp presses her face up next to Jerry's. "I hear the pilot saw lights on the dark side," she murmurs.

Jerry backs away from the viewport, annoyed. "Not necessarily a bad sign," he says, and moves toward the row of gleaming black planetary probes fastened to the far wall of the cargo bay. "Wildfires, volcanic vents. At worst, the feeble efforts of some primitive species."

"Maybe so," Phthsspitty-snapp allows, sidling up alongside Jerry. "But earlier, at the snack bar on 2A, I heard someone say the lights were pretty darn white, and there were huge clusters along the coastlines and way inland."

How do you annoy me? Jerry thinks. Let me count the ways. As staff scientist, he was supposed to have been debriefed by a pilot or a member of his team within minutes of the establishment of orbit. By now he should have a wealth of data about the planet below, and if he chooses to be generous, he will share bits with his little protégé here. Getting news from an underling is bad enough. Why does the news have to be annoying, too? "I guess we'll find out," is all he says, and he opens the control orb tethered to his elbow by a thin green wire.

"I have pretty extensive training in the use of that thing," Phthsspitty-snapp volunteers, hovering at Jerry's front shoulder.

Jerry just grunts, his fingers quivering along the glassy surface of the orb. A human observer would think the control orb looked like a glass Millefiori paperweight and perhaps would be dazzled by the vibrations of Jerry's fingers on its surface, not understanding how the subtle movements could possibly convey information. Massaging the orb, Jerry recalls the readings taken by the ship as it approached Grawgraw-3. He matches the settings of the planetary probe in front of him to Grawgraw-3's ambient temperature, planetary gravity, and atmospheric pressure. He checks the probe's audio and video feeds, then runs automated checks of its sensory instruments and propulsion system. Closing the orb, he studies the probe one last time, flicks a speck of dust from its midsection, then turns away with a satisfied nod.

And bumps right into Phthsspitty-snapp. "Are you sure this planet is that temperate?" she asks, blinking rapidly.

"Just going by the preliminary readings," Jerry says, placing his front hand on her rear shoulder as he moves past her purposefully.

"But it wouldn't hurt to set it for a broader range," she says, trotting along behind him. "At least initially."

Time to get pedantic. Jerry stops, facing Phthsspitty-snapp. "Look. As you know, that probe can tolerate extreme heat and cold, no matter what the settings are. But it operates more efficiently when it 'knows' what temperatures to 'expect,' roughly. That's all it is. And as you know, the settings can be changed remotely in the event that we discover this planet holds surprises. Understood?"

"Yes sir." She gives him an apologetic smile, and he realizes how young she is. Of course it is her first planetary mission, and she feels the same excitement and anticipation he felt years earlier on the mission to Andromomo-12. Just like her, he imagined the analysis would show evidence of sentient life-forms. Like him, she would have to be satisfied with the dull, everyday truth that emerged in 99 out of 100 planetary analyses. "Come on," he says. "Let's launch the probe."

preceding product sample has had any deleterious effect, you agree to hold the creator of Oily blameless and that continued use of Oily on your part may be ill-advised.

IV. DESCRIPTION

A. Classification: Oily is a book. This document serves as a Terms of Use Agreement for all versions, editions, and copies of Oily, whether they be electronic, non-electronic, further printings, further editions, special "Now a Major Motion Picture" editions, audio editions, young adult/juvenile/children's editions, and all other iterations, no matter how unlikely it may be that any iteration aside from the free electronic and reasonably priced print-on-demand versions ever be produced. Oily's creator hopes that at least a few people besides friends and family members might read Oily someday.

B. Genre: Oily is a novel. As noted in Article II, it is a work of imaginative fiction whose similarities to reality are coincidental. For purposes of classification by indexers, librarians, booksellers, academicians, and talk-show hosts, Oily may be identified as science fiction ("sci-fi"). However, Oily is not "hard-core" sci-fi, a la Robert Heinlein® and Larry Niven™, whose names are used with permission of the executors of their respective estates. Indexers et al. may wish to classify Oily as literary fiction or literary science fiction ("lit sci-fi"), shelving or listing it alongside works by Margaret Atwood, Kurt Vonnegut, Marge Piercy, Ray Bradbury, et al. The creator of Oily makes no claims regarding the proper classification of the product and reserves the right to allow Oily to be classified as one-of-a-kind. For the time being, of course, indexers et al. are unlikely to find the need classify Oily at all, seeing as how its creator has decided to make it available for free as an e-book and at a reasonable cost as a print-on-demand book, which would seem to consign Oily to the dustbin of history—let's be realistic—despite the fact that some other self-published novels have caught on, generated buzz, and been picked up by traditional publishers. The creator of Oily supposes that some will classify him as one of those jokers, so numerous these days, who thinks he can write a novel—who thinks that just anyone can write a novel. And that it only takes about a year: you get an idea, you write out the story, it gets published. How about ten years?

C. Characters: Oily contains a cast of fictitious human and alien characters including Warren, Penny, Jerry, Phthsspitty-snapp (all of whom are introduced in Article III), Gravy (see Article V), and Hmmm (see Article V). Other fictitious figures are named but hardly qualify as characters.

D. Setting: The narrative conveyed by Oily takes place in a variety of settings, including but not limited to a small house in New Orleans; the interior of a car; outer space; in, on, or near offshore or onshore oil rigs; underwater; way up in the sky; the Nigerian delta; and a beach in Grand Isle, Louisiana.

E. Narrative: Oily depicts a series of events that comprise a narrative ("story"). Events depicted include (but are not limited to) conversations, discoveries, collisions, accidents, epiphanies, arguments, sabotage, and a pie cooling on a countertop.

Oily's events are depicted in sentences, which are comprised of words. The narrative which is the primary feature of Oily begins with the character Warren entering his modest home in New Orleans, Louisiana, and showing his wife Penny a mysterious black object he found on a nearby levee (see Article II), a few hours after an alien with the "ridiculously human name" (according to a certain literary agent) of Jerry prepares a planetary probe 188 miles above Earth with the assistance of an alien intern with the ridiculously alien name of Phthsspitty-snapp. Oily continues with Penny telling Warren, "You need to call Dr. Neufchatel" the moment he reappears, steaming tea and toast in hand. Warren subsequently rolls his eyes, lips tight, and uses the tea mug to push aside some medicine bottles before setting it down. He sits·on the bed, taking Penny's hand in both of his. The narrative continues with a brief dialogue (see IV.I below):

"I know what I saw."
"Look, you've been under a lot of stress with all of this." She glances around the bedroom at the meds, barf bowls, and bandages. "I know it's hard on you. You're not getting enough sleep. Maybe you need a higher dose, or a lower dose."
He shakes his head. "I'm not taking this because I was delusional or hearing voices," he reminds her. "I wasn't crazy, and I'm still not. Just anxious."

"Maybe it's a rare side effect." Penny stretches for her smart phone and starts thumbing buttons. "I bet it is. I'll look it up. Dr. Neufchatel can switch you to a different medication."

Warren lowers his voice. "I was going to leave it out there," he says. "Just another interesting piece of junk, but so what? I picked it up, looked it over, tossed it back in the grass." He talks the way he talks at night after they get in bed, pushing words he would never say to anyone else through her hair and into her ears. "I was watching a least tern fly over the canal when I saw it move out of the corner of my eye. It lifted up off the grass and kind of rotated slowly, then drifted up close to my face."

Penny's thumbs stop moving and she peers over her glasses at the screen of her phone. "Headaches, nausea, constipation, diarrhea, dizziness, lethargy, hyperactivity, euphoria, depression, hair loss, appetite increase or decrease, weight loss, weight gain, and tinnitus. Nothing about delusions or hallucinations."

"I felt the hair stand up on the back of my neck. You ever felt that? It really happens. Then it rotated away from me and started moving off. I grabbed it before it could get away." He shook his head. "I decided I must be dreaming, but so far I haven't woken up."

"Ooh, I'm woozy," Penny groans, sinking down into her pillows.

"The tea!" Warren takes the mug and presses it into her hands. "You took the meds?"

She nods, and Warren watches her cradle the tea, wincing and taking tentative sips. Her light brown hair is greasy, spread in clumps over the pillow, and the skin all around her eyes looks gloomy and bruised. Her lips are colorless, but he sees her walking along the beach, plump and rosy, thick ponytail shining in the sun as it swings from side to side. How long ago was that? It had been a scorching day, one of the first of that summer. Less than a year? Looking away for a moment, he can see it more clearly: Penny standing up from the sand to walk down to the water in her purple dress, resting her hands on top of her head for a moment, kicking at the sand idly. The next question, of course, is how long it will be until she glows like that again. Maybe if he stayed home in the mornings instead of seeking solace out on the levee, that day would come sooner. He should be getting up early not to walk but to write, to hole up in his study and work on that novel he started last year, to be right there in the next room when Penny wakes up. And then maybe he'd rush in not to show her things he'd found on the levee but to tell her he'd finished the novel, he'd sold the novel, the novel was now in stores. He leans forward to kiss her pained face. "You're right," he says. "I should call Dr. Neufchatel."

Penny nods, eyes closed.

"You going to throw up?" he asks. "You need a Phenergan™?" She shakes her head, but he puts the pink throw-up bowl on the bed anyway. "I'll get a wet washcloth." And throw the black acorn out the door while I'm at it. Whatever it is, and whatever it can do, they just don't have room for it in their lives.

Just one problem. The windowsill over the kitchen sink, where he laid the black acorn while the tea water boiled, is empty.

F. Point of view: Oily's narration employs multiple third-person limited omniscient points of view. By clicking "Agree" below, you solemnly swear to tolerate the anonymous narrator's ability to relate circumstances, events, and dialogue of various characters in various settings, even when these events may be happening simultaneously thousands of miles apart. Furthermore, you accept the narrator's ability to relate the inaudible thoughts, emotions, and sensations of a limited set of fictitious characters, namely Warren, Jerry, and occasionally Phthsspitty-snapp. In addition, you promise to refrain from wondering who the narrator could be or considering the narrator to be a character with any significant role to play in the narrative itself. In return, the creator of Oily accepts the obligation to employ multiple third-person limited omniscient points of view responsibly, consistently, and clearly. The creator of Oily is not just some joker who up and wrote a novel and published it himself because it was crappy and no publisher would touch it with a ten-foot pole. No, the creator of Oily knows how to handle third-person limited omniscient point of view because he studied writing in college, even earning an advanced degree. And the creator of Oily published stories in a few small literary journals, some of which were actually printed and mailed and handled by their readers. He also wrote several perfectly publishable stories which never appeared in any publication, and of all of the stories he has written, some were in first-person point of view, some in third-person limited omniscient. But there are no guarantees in this business. Just because you mastered points of view and know how to write sparkling dialogue and have an MFA, that doesn't mean agents and editors will come fawning around you, handing you book contracts on silver platters. They're finicky, and they're also inundated with proposals and manuscripts and pleas from tens of thousands of writers. But the creator of Oily decided that agents and editors only slow things down and get in the way, coming between a book and its readers, such that by the time a book about the worst oil spill in American history gets past agents and editors and reaches readers, everyone has pretty much forgotten about the worst oil spill in American history or at least doesn't care about it as much as they did a few years earlier.

At any rate, whenever possible, accounts of events separated by time and/or distance will be kept separate. Such separation will generally (though not exclusively) be accomplished and signaled by the skipping of lines ("white space") between scenes with different points of view. Scenes in which both Warren and Jerry appear shall use paragraph breaks to signal shifts in points of view (see Article IV.F). For example, the scene ending with, "The windowsill over the kitchen sink, where he had laid the black acorn while the tea water heated, is empty" shall be followed by white space, after which the subsequent scene shall begin with the sentence, "Jerry the alien has a bad feeling about this planet," in which the narrator identifies an inaudible thought of a fictitious character. It should be noted that the inaudible thoughts of only one fictitious character, namely Jerry, are depicted in the remainder of the scene, despite the presence of another fictitious character, namely Phthsspitty-snapp, viz.:

First the lights on the dark side, if Phthsspitty-snapp is to be believed, and now the probe is on the fritz. After landfall, he took his time rebooting sensors, starting with the gas spectrometer, and the readouts were mostly as expected, except for a worrisome amount of carbon dioxide and some as-yet-unidentified inorganic particulate matter. Pressure, gravitation, and temperature readings brought no surprises.

Phthsspitty-snapp sits beside him at the probe's control console, unblinkingly absorbing every flick of every switch and every quiver of every readout. "Hmm," she says once in a while, "hmm" as in "Hmm, that's intriguing." Annoyed, Jerry delays opening up the audio and video sensors. He fiddles with this and that, takes a few meaningless notes. He has always saved audio and video for last anyway, in part because of his training as a scientist, which taught him that sensory input is not as informative or reliable as samples and measurements, and that they can be deceptive. But the tourist in Jerry saves them for last because they are the best. With the flick of a switch, he can reveal the sights and sounds of a planet no one has visited for millions of years. New colors and shapes will appear with dozens of noises loud and small, beautiful and harsh.

Phthsspitty-snapp shifts restlessly and finally can't wait any longer. "Audio and video...?" she says.

"What do you think of this planet so far?" Jerry asks. "Based on what you know."

"Well," she says. "It's rather small compared to Xxzzrrrva. It rotates almost ten times per Xxzzrrrvan day, orbits its sun almost thirty times per Xxzzrrrvan year. A stable atmosphere of mostly nitrogen and oxygen. Little volcanic and seismic activity. Lots of water, ice at the poles. Evidence of plentiful aquatic and terrestrial vegetable matter, possibility of animal life-forms."

"Yeah, yeah. All very textbook. But what do you think we'll find?" Jerry busies himself with fine-tuning temperature settings, as if her answer makes no difference to him.

"Honestly? Sentient beings. Lots of them."

"What kind of sentient beings?"

"The kind that knows how to make artificial light, if nothing else."

"And...?"

"Anything beyond that would be sheer speculation," Phthsspitty-snapp says dutifully.

Jerry smiles, nodding. With a raise of the eyebrows, he reaches for the glowing rectangle that will power up video and audio sensors. Just as he stretches to touch it, something jostles the probe, then lifts it, turning it this way and that on every axis.

"What's happening?" Phthsspitty-snapp asks.

"Temperature rise," Jerry says, scanning the displays. "Organic oils and salts." This will be one of *those* expeditions. His reports back to Xxzzrrrva will disappoint the Exploratory Board, at least a little and maybe a lot. He can only hope it will not go down in history as one of those very bad expeditions, like the one to Bloofo-4 generations ago that found only desert, toxic seas, and basalt, or the one to Ti that found vast numbers of warring machines controlled by vicious carnivores. Those explorers barely made it out alive. Planets like those are part of the reason Xxzzrrrva is in such a desperate condition. One out of a hundred expeditions seems to be a disaster. What are the chances that Jerry's 29th (and Phthsspitty-snapp's first) will be the bad one?

Now the motion sensors show the probe undergoing a rhythmic jostling as it moves slowly across the planet's surface. Jerry makes sure Phthsspitty-snapp is watching as he instructs the probe to sample the substrate on which it rests. "Plant fiber," she muses quietly.

"Conclusion?"

Phthsspitty-snapp shakes her head, afraid to say it out loud. Jerry says it for her. "The probe appears to have either landed upon or been picked up by a large life-form, which is now carrying it to an unknown destination." *And if you panic now, we'll never get along.*

Phthsspitty-snapp grins, eyeing the controls for the audio and video sensors.

Jerry makes her wait. "And the plant fiber?" he asks.

"Where was it they found a species of muscular cactus-dogs...?"

"Globard," he says. "Seventy years ago. Or...?"

Phthsspitty-snapp squints as if scanning inner memory-banks, then shakes her head.

"The carnivores of Ti...?" Jerry hints.

"...Clothed themselves with mats of boiled plant fiber."

Nodding, Jerry turns on the audio. The only sound picked up by the probe is the constant friction of fiber against microphone. He figures video won't show much at this point, but he turns it on anyway. Nothing happens at first, and then an error message pops up on the display, telling him that he must download the latest version of the video software to proceed. Cursing the mothers of Xxzzrrrva's software moguls, Jerry clicks "OK." Phthsspitty-snapp laughs, and Jerry decides she might be tolerable company after all.

Of course after the software downloads and Jerry clicks "INSTALL," a window containing vast shoals of text pops up. BEFORE INSTALLING THIS SOFTWARE, YOU MUST AGREE TO THE TERMS SPECIFIED BELOW. CLICK "AGREE" TO CONTINUE....

"Aren't you going to read that?" Phthsspitty-snapp jokes.

"No one reads those things," Jerry says, and clicked AGREE.

THE ABOVE EXCERPT REPRESENTS A TYPICAL PRESENTATION OF POINT OF VIEW IN OILY; HOWEVER, THE CREATOR OF OILY MAKES NO GUARANTEES REGARDING VARIATIONS IN THE PRESENTATION OF POINT OF VIEW WITHIN THE NOVEL.

G. Characterization: As creator of Oily, Warren Avon is committed to supplying a rich experience for readers. Isn't that what good fiction does? Doesn't it hypnotize readers into a sort of trance in which they visualize the story and even hear the thoughts of the characters? It was that hypnotic state that Warren Avon loved as an avidly reading child, and it was a desire to conduct the same sort of sorcery that made him want to be a writer. In keeping with the commitment to creating a rich experience, major fictitious characters appearing within Oily shall be "three dimensional" rather than "two-dimensional." Every effort shall be made to create the illusion that major fictitious characters are actual, particularized individuals, despite the fact that each of them is wholly the product of the creator's imagination (see Article II). Lesser and/or minor characters may appear "flat" in comparison to major characters; however, every effort has been made to avoid presenting any character as a type (e.g., the wacky neighbor, cynical cop, or eager cub reporter), with the possible exception of Councilor Hmmm (the imperious villain with the aristocratic accent).

As reader, you understand that the creator of Oily may characterize fictitious characters by showing one of them standing in the bedroom doorway, twisting his wedding band, and the other raising her head from a cloud of nausea to squint at him from behind her hair. Both characters in this case may be further characterized by a conversational exchange in which she says, "Did you get it?" and he replies, "Actually, no," at which point she asks, "Why not?" and he says casually, "Funny thing. I couldn't find it. Isn't that weird?" The exchange continues:

"Couldn't find it?"

"Right. It just disappeared."

"Why didn't you just get another one?"

"Get another one?"

"Get another one."

"You think there would be another one?"

"Jeez, Warren! Now you're scaring me. I'll call him myself. We've got a whole stack of them in the closet!"

Note that accounts of a major character's inaudible thoughts also characterize, as here where Warren reflects that so far Penny's meds have not addled her much, except when she is sleepy, which she isn't now. He studies her, head cocked. "Whole stack in the closet...really?"

"Are you looking for the striped one? I don't care which one it is, so long as it's damp, And cool. I want a cool one, not a hot one."

"Oh, the washcloth! In the linen closet! I forgot! Hang on a minute!" Within thirty seconds he is sitting by her on the bed, cool damp washcloth in hand. He holds it to her forehead, wipes her cheeks and neck. Penny lies back, closing her eyes.

"What were *you* talking about?" she murmurs.

"Oh, me? Nothing."

She keeps her eyes closed, and for a moment Warren thinks she is drifting off—always a good sign when she feels bad, and an even better sign at the moment. He feels a little like a trout when the line tugging at its jaw goes slack. "No, really," she says. "What were you talking about?" The line tightens.

"I got sidetracked on the way to get your washcloth," he says. "I was looking for a book."

"Which one?"

"Which one?" Warren glances around the room. "*Anything You Say Can and Will Be Used Against You* by Laurie Drummond," he says. "Oh, look—here it is!" He frees the blue and yellow hardback from its place between the lamp and an old water glass.

Penny shakes her head against the pillow, eyes closed. "I don't know about you," she says.

H. Chronology: Like many (but not all) novels, Oily presents a sequence of events in roughly chronological order. The creator of Oily makes no guarantees that all events are presented in a strict chronology but shall make reasonable efforts to indicate clearly the temporal relationships between events (which does not constitute an obligation to provide exact dates and/or times for any events). Whenever events described in the course of the narrative occur simultaneously in whole or in part, they shall be presented consecutively.

Readers of the TOU should have noted that the consecutive scenes that begin the novel are temporally out of sync, as Jerry and Phthsspitty-snapp's preparation of the planetary probe aboard the Xxzzrrrvan mother ship takes place hours prior to Warren and Penny's first conversation regarding the black acorn. As a qualified reader of Oily (See Article II), you have an obligation to tolerate and understand such disjunctions and to trust that the creator of Oily finds them occasionally necessary, particularly as the narrative begins. Additionally, it should be noted that synchronization is achieved in the following passage from Oily:

Jerry finally powers up the video sensor. The jostling continued throughout the downloading and installing of the updated software, then became intermittent and random.

Phthsspitty-snapp leans forward eagerly as the video screen's glow brightens. "Damn it," Jerry says.

"Cool," Phthsspitty-snapp says.

The screen shows the interior of an enormous alien shelter, surprisingly geometric and crisp, all principal surfaces meeting at perfect right angles. A large sleeping platform dominates the room, covered in colorful fabrics whose composition he will determine later by sampling. The floor looks to be made of shiny organic panels. A large architectonic object stands in one corner. It has several storage compartments and a shiny upright panel above. All very alien. Small architectonic structures stand on either side of the sleeping platform, objects of various heights standing on them. Light comes through two large fabric-covered openings in the wall.

Jerry takes all of this in with an expert eye in the first few seconds, after which the view swivels roughly. "Whoa," Phthsspitty-snapp says. "Aliens." He has trouble categorizing the life-forms as one of the aliens turns the probe this way and that with a nearly hairless appendage. The video feed becomes a jumble, and he notes what information he can. At least two jointed appendages. Large head. Binocular vision. Flat, squarish teeth in a wide mouth. Cranial hair of considerable length. One of the life-forms is nearly prone on the sleeping-platform, the other vertical. Audio is picking up the aliens' vocalizations, a series of rapid hoots and hisses, with the occasional hum. The sounds have a wandering rhythm, speeding and slowing as needed, but few patterns. The probes' processors will determine whether the sounds are lingual, and clearly they are. Jerry has studied many languages, from the clicking dental codes of Djuangi's polar felines to the majestic songs of Crabidabuotz's primitive fungi, and every time he hears a new one he marvels. What a shame that these life forms have reached a stage where they burn massive quantities of natural resources to generate the electromagnetic charges detected by the probe's sensors. The charges power illuminators at least, and probably other devices as well.

Phthsspitty-snapp leans closer to the video display. "Elegant architecture," she remarks.

Jerry just grunts, and the video feed becomes a collage of motion again, then goes mostly dark. The sampling lance reports organic fibers. After a moment, the screen brightens, showing the interior of another chamber in the alien shelter. An alien appendage places the probe on a narrow horizontal surface in front of an opening to the outdoors. Jerry jabs the substrate with the sampling lance. Organic cellulose, with a resinous coating.

"Everything's organic," Phthsspitty-snapp says.

"So far."

"That's a good sign, right?"

Jerry doesn't answer. He watches the video display, catching a glimpse of the alien's movements about the chamber once in a while. He doesn't dare move the probe to get a better view until the motion sensor shows that the alien has left this chamber of the evidently multi-chambered shelter. He watches a blob representing Warren bounce around the motion sensor's screen.

Phthsspitty-snapp clears her throat. "There's an alert on the communications display," she says. "Looks like you've got a high priority space-mail."

Jerry doesn't take his eyes off the motion sensor. " Who from?"

"The Exploratory Board."

Jerry sighs. "Open it."

"The 19th Federal Exploratory Board of the Xxzzrrrvan Union congratulates you on your successful navigation to

Grawgraw-3. Your safe arrival is testament to the navigational—
.'"

"Skip to the fourth paragraph. The rest is just boilerplate."

"Okay. It's real short: 'We anticipate transmission of your preliminary report, complete with sampling data and a tentative exploitation plan, by noon Tuesday.'"

"Shoot. How do they expect me to compile a report like that in one day when I've got my hands full with the probe?"

"I can draft the report," Phthsspitty-snapp says. "We've already got some sampling data."

"Here we go." The blob that is Warren moves through an opening and out into a short interior corridor whose outlines glow on the motion sensor. Jerry expertly guides the probe from the windowsill to a high corner near the opening through which the alien has just passed. He widens the view on the video sensor and leans forward to study the chamber below. It bristles with objects and equipment laid out on horizontal surfaces. Below the windowsill are dual metallic depressions edged with shiny fittings. He can see numerous storage compartments, large and small, about the room. "Looks like a variety of materials," Jerry mutters. "Vitreous, metallic, organic. Possible thermoplastics."

"Check," Phthsspitty-snapp says, typing rapidly.

Jerry makes the sampling lance jab the ceiling and wall in their high corner. "Walls of soft mineral under a layer of crudely processed cellulose, coated with a semi-inorganic glaze."

"Check."

"Stop saying 'check.' This is not a movie."

"They told us to say 'check.'"

"I'll bet they also told you to do what your supervisor asked you to do. Just say 'okay' once in a while, but not very often."

"Check," Phthsspitty-snapp says, and gives Jerry such a grin when he turns angrily that he has to laugh.

[POINT OF VIEW SHIFT. OILY ITSELF WILL INDICATE SUCH SHIFTS ONLY WITH WHITE SPACE]

Penny reconfigures the pillows so that she can sit up against the headboard. "Book or laptop?" Warren asks.

"Laptop."

He takes the computer from its slot between the bedside table and the bed, setting it on her thighs. All the while he is sneaking glances around the room, searching for the black acorn. What the hell could it be? Some newfangled remote-control toy? Some random plastic thing that he'd simply misplaced? Maybe its little flight out on the levee was a dream—he could have nodded off for a moment without realizing it. Maybe Penny is right and the pills he's been taking for anxiety are giving him hallucinations. Nothing else makes sense.

He hears a voice. "Warren?" it says softly. "Warren, honey?" It is Penny, holding up one end of the laptop cord. "Could you plug it in for me?"

Once Penny has gotten settled, he sits back beside her and takes a more thorough survey of the bedroom. No black acorn on the dresser or on either bedside table. He kicks the covers surreptitiously, moving the wrinkles and folds. Stretching, he knocks a medicine bottle off the table, says "Oops," and gets down on the floor for a quick look under the bed, finding only clumps of dust and the old headphones. Standing, he quickly checks the rest of the floor, then moves out into the hallway purposefully. Nothing out there. Same results in the study, the bathroom, and the dining room. And that's all there is to their little starter home. "Here acorn, acorn, acorn," Warren says under his breath, just to make himself laugh. He goes back to the kitchen and looks in the drawers, in the refrigerator, and under the bread-box. He puts his hand down into the disposer and feels around. Nothing but gritty slime.

"Warren!" Penny calls. "Warren, get in here!"

[POINT OF VIEW SHIFT. OILY ITSELF WILL INDICATE SUCH SHIFTS ONLY WITH WHITE SPACE] [CONTEXT CLUES INDICATE THAT THE FOLLOWING SCENE OCCURS BEFORE AND/OR DURING PRECEDING SCENE]

Jerry guides the probe down to the blue horizontal surface beside the metallic depressions, keeping it close to the wall. "What time is it?" he asks Phthsspitty-snapp.

"Xxzzrrrva time?"

He nods, deploying the sampling lance.

"Forty-seven o'clock. So that's...twenty eight hours before the preliminary report is due."

"Not why I was asking," Jerry lies. "Bad news," he adds.

Phthsspitty-snapp leans closer to the display. "Phenolic resin. So?"

"Typically manufactured from isopropyl benzene...?"

"Chemistry was never my strong suit," she says.

"...A constituent of petroleum."

"Oh. Damn. What are we going to do?"

"They call it planetary analysis for a reason," Jerry says. "We'll keep going." He lifts the probe from the blue surface and moves on to sample the metallic depressions (iron alloy), the transparent opening (vitreous silica), the exteriors of storage compartments (organic cellulose with a synthetic polyurethane coating), and a thick square of fabric (woven fibers of polyethylene terephthalate). Moving the probe cautiously into the hallway with one eye on the motion detector, he scans a vitreous/metallic device in the center of the ceiling, confirming that it is most likely an illuminator connected to a vast and complex electromagnetic delivery system that weaves its way throughout the house. He nudges the probe down the hall and through the opening into another chamber, which turns out to be the one with the sleeping platform. Just one of the alien life-forms lies on the platform. "I think it's safe to assume any glossy brown surface is organic cellulose," Jerry tells Phthsspitty-snapp. "But why don't you run a comparison, see if it's all from the same plant species."

"Check," Phthsspitty-snapp says, and before Jerry can rebuke her, the alien starts to scream.

[POINT OF VIEW SHIFT. OILY ITSELF WILL INDICATE SUCH SHIFTS ONLY WITH WHITE SPACE] [CONTEXT CLUES INDICATE THAT THE FOLLOWING SCENE OCCURS IMMEDIATELY AFTER PRECEDING SCENE]

Warren pulls his hand from the garbage disposer and runs to the bedroom, wiping his hands on his jeans. Penny has her legs drawn up, her book clutched in both hands. She stares aghast at the ceiling. "Is that a roach?" she asks. "I can't find my glasses! It looks huge! Get it!"

Warren lunges toward the dresser, grabbing a magazine, and leaps up onto the bed. By the time he looks at the ceiling, he has the May issue of *Real Simple* rolled up tight, and he brandishes it fearlessly, prepared to locate, pursue, and destroy whatever large insect is threatening his homestead. When he sees the black acorn hovering above the doorway, he freezes, then drops his hands to his sides.

"Is it a roach?" Penny asks. "Don't tell me it's a spider...."

Warren hesitates, then re-brandishes the rolled-up magazine. "Yes," he says. "It's a roach. I'll get it!" And he leaps off the bed, weapon held high.

I. Dialogue: Oily makes use of dialogue between fictitious characters. By no stretch of the imagination (including but not limited to speculation, inference, and guesswork) does the creator of Oily ascertain that statements, questions, phrases, and/or words exchanged between characters are reported as they occurred in any actual circumstance, situation, or happenstance.

The creator of Oily makes every effort to ensure that dialogue is presented according to the conventions and traditions of American fiction. Direct quotation of fictional characters shall be signaled by the use of double quotation marks (" "). Speakers shall frequently but not always be identified by the use of tag lines such as "she said" and "said Jerry." As reader you have an obligation to keep track of who is saying what, whether or not tag lines are provided. Paragraph breaks shall be utilized in most cases to distinguish speakers from one another. Furthermore, the creator of Oily does not subscribe to Elmore Leonard's recommendation to use only forms of the verb "to say" in tag lines. However, due to the current popularity of Mr. Leonard's proscription in literary circles (including but not limited to writers, editors, agents, and publishers), the creator of Oily will make infrequent use of more descriptive verbs, including but not limited to "murmur," "declare," "swear," and/or "gasp." Reasonable efforts have been made to avoid annoying verbs such as "affirm" and "aver." Writers must be sensitive to such preferences.

Long ago the trend in fiction was to use misspellings and apostrophes to approximate characters' accents, leading to absurdities such as, "Noah, murm, ah doan righ'ly b'lieve it dun bin chopt douin yit!" Times changed, and no one would be caught dead doing that. A writer could pen a brilliant book, but too much *affirming* and *murmuring* in the first chapter and agents won't touch it, and so the writer keeps querying and querying and the agents keep rejecting and rejecting, and no one tells the writer that he or she will never get through, no matter how beautiful or hilarious or upsetting their tale, unless their characters start *saying* things to one another. And people don't understand how long all of that can take, first querying ten perfectly suited agents with a carefully polished letter, waiting for most of them to respond, then querying ten or twenty more agents who are probably pretty much suitable, waiting for them, querying more, waiting, querying, waiting. It takes a couple of years, and it's dispiriting. And if a writer gets an agent, the writer probably has to wait while the agent sends the work around to editors, and then wait for the agent to wait to hear from the editor and on and on, and if an editor does decide to publish the book, the writer has to wait another year or two for the book to drift through the whole publishing process, so that by the time the book hits the shelves the writer can hardly remember what it was about. So it's understandable that a writer might decide to just chop through the whole Gordian mess and take his book right to the people via the internet.

Readers are hereby warned and forewarned that Oily makes relatively extensive use of dialogue. Dialogue serves various narrative purposes, including but not limited to characterization (see Article III. G), advancing the story, and providing transition. The creator of Oily neither guarantees nor promises that every line of dialogue serves a single purpose; it is possible that certain lines of dialogue serve multiple purposes and/or no particular or identifiable purpose. As reader you accept the possibility that mere whim on the part of the creator of Oily may play a role in dialogue. Before clicking "Agree" below, readers should carefully read the following excerpt, which demonstrates Oily's use of the conventions of dialogue:

As the multi-colored cylinder of processed cellulose fills the video display, Jerry slams the probe into reverse, which would have been the right move if there weren't a wall right behind it. The end of the cylinder catches the nose of the probe as the alien descends, appendage outstretched, and the probe tumbles for a moment, gyros confused. It hits the floor right in front of the now crouching alien, whose bare appendage unfolds quickly, digits closing on the fuselage of the probe.

[DIALOGUE:]
"I've got it!" Warren says.
"Ew! With your hand?" Penny has by now found her glasses. "Go flush it down the toilet! Quick!"
"Right!" He planned to throw it out the front door, but the toilet is closer. Why not?
[ADVANCES NARRATIVE; CHARACTERIZES "PENNY"]

Meanwhile, at the control console, Jerry's heart rate has risen. "Don't panic," he says to Phthsspitty-snapp, staring at the shifting pink smudges on the video display. He glances at her face, which shows no trace of panic. She wears the smile of someone watching a thrilling sci-fi movie.

The motion sensor shows that the probe has entered a relatively small chamber that it has not yet visited. The alien releases the probe, which tumbles briefly. Jerry catches glimpses of glossy blue walls, hanging rectangles of fabric, and some sort of white fixtures before the probe falls into a large white bowl of water. Alerts pop up on video: AQUATIC ENVIRONMENT. The light dims as the alien shuts a large lid on top of the bowl. The probe sinks slowly to the bottom.

[DIALOGUE:]
"What's it trying to do?" Phthsspitty-snapp laughs.

Jerry is busy deploying the sampling lance. "Hard, processed mineral. Significant bacteria counts." He is interrupted by an oceanic sound, and the water begins to spin, carrying the probe down into a darker passage. Jerry shrugs, letting the water carry the probe along. Bacteria concentrations rise steeply. He taps a button, and the probe's illuminators shine on the rough metallic walls of a circular passageway full of rushing water.

"Yuck," Phthsspitty-snapp says. "Do you think this is...."

Jerry nods. "Waste disposal. Not a bad solution, though I think Xxzzrrrva's is superior."

[ADVANCES NARRATIVE; CHARACTERIZES "JERRY" AND "PHTHSSPITTY-SNAPP"]

Warren cautiously lifts the toilet seat, relieved to find nothing but water and white porcelain beneath it. He hangs his head for a moment, relieved and baffled. He suppresses his bafflement, simply deciding that he will never know what that object was. The important thing is that it is gone. Halfway through washing his hands, he wonders why he is washing his hands.

Fortunately the probe the Exploratory Board provided is state-of-the-art. Jerry tries out a new feature, Rapid Reverse, which acts as a rewind button, taking the probe quickly back through the path it has just followed, replicating every twist and quiver at high speed. It makes a good escape key, and Jerry taps it once. The probe backs into the current flowing down the metallic passageway, picking up speed as it comes closer to the mineral bowl.

Warren is drying his hands when the black acorn shoots up out of the toilet in a fountain of spray. "Gah!" he shouts, slapping at the acorn with the hand towel. It clatters to the floor, and he pounces on it again.

[NOT EXACTLY DIALOGUE]

"Not again," Jerry groans, then sighs. "Might as well take a sample."

Before Warren can take two steps toward the front door, the acorn stings him, giving him a sharp little needle-prick that is just enough to make him drop it on the bathroom floor. He throws the towel at the acorn, steps into the hall, and slams the door.

[DIALOGUE—THE FOLLOWING SECTION INCLUDES PARALLEL DIALOGUES INVOLVING A TOTAL OF FOUR CHARACTERS. THE MAKER AND PROVIDERS OF OILY MAKE NO GUARANTEE AGAINST CONFUSION AND/OR ANNOYANCE]

"Warren?" Penny calls. "What's going on?"

"What's going on?" Warren says, studying his palm. No blood or anything, but he sure felt a jab in the meat below his thumb.

"Read that to me while I find a way out," Jerry says to Phthsspitty-snapp.

"Carbon-based life form...oxygenated blood...high sodium, iron, and calcium content...."

"Did you flush it down the toilet?" Penny calls to Warren.

"Yes, I did," he replies, deciding not to mention that it unflushed itself.

"Good," she says, her voice close. Warren looks up from his palm and finds Penny swaying in the hallway, one hand on the wall. She looks meaningfully at the door behind him. "Is it safe to go in there?"

"Safe to—no. No, it's not—it's just kind of a mess. Yeah, let me just—." He squeezes past her and trots into the kitchen. He opens a drawer, picks up a strainer, shakes his head, and opens a cabinet.

Jerry sets the video display to its widest view, piloting the probe slowly around the perimeter of the bathroom. "No openings," he says.

"Will it fit under the door?" Phthsspitty-snapp asks.

"Check and see."

Phthsspitty-snapp taps the video display, then fiddles with a flat dial. "Insufficient clearance," she says.

Jerry laughs. "Insufficient clearance. That's very official. You can just say, 'It won't fit.'"

"Roger that, captain."

Warren gives Penny an apologetic smile as he slips past her holding a plastic container they usually use for leftover rice or pasta. "What's that for?" she asks. "Is it still in there?"

"No," he says innocently. "I mean, I don't think so. But I want to make sure it went down. You know how sometimes they float and swim around. And this is just in case—you know, it might be the flying kind."

"Well, hurry up," Penny says, knees together. "I need to get back in bed."

Jerry eases the probe down into the white mineral bowl. "Where do you suppose it leads to?" he says, staring at the shadowy cavern at the bottom.

"Depends on the sophistication of their waste disposal system," Phthsspitty-snapp points out. "Body of water? Incinerator?"

"Hmm." With a few taps, he instructs the probe to replay its recent voyage down the toilet on the video display, and he and Phthsspitty-snapp both lean forward to study it. Neither of them notice the activity on the motion sensor.

Warren winks at Penny and slips into the bathroom, heart pounding. He kicks the hand towel across the floor. Nothing. Plastic container in one hand, lid in the other, he advances, peering into the sink, then the bathtub. A dark shadow glimmers in the toilet—the acorn, hovering just below the rim. Wincing, he gets down low and holds his breath, arms out. The acorn hangs perfectly still. Warren lunges, clapping the container and lid together over the acorn.

"What was that?" Jerry says, and flicks back to live video. Alarms blare as an external force moves the probe this way and that and it bumps against hard surfaces. Jerry's first glance of video makes him think the probe is underwater or in a dense fog. He can make out the alien's blue clothing close by. Echolocation shows that the probe is in a squarish box, and the sampling lance reports that it is made from polyethylene. This polyethylene is translucent, reducing the world to fuzzy patches of color.

"It captured the probe," Phthsspitty-snapp says. "Want me to boot up the weapons system?"

"Of course not! Is that what they teach at the Institute these days?"

She shrugs. "Not really."

"Is it in there?" Penny asks as Warren rushes past her with the container. "What are you doing?"

"Just...tossing it outside." He hurries to the front door before she can ask anything else. The green heat of day comes as a shock, and he stands for a moment in blazing sun before descending the four concrete steps of the front stoop. He holds the container firmly, one hand ready to peel off the lid, arm cocked to fling the acorn toward the street so he can forget about it and get on with his life, the rest of which he will spend puzzling over the four-inch black object that flew noiselessly and gave him a sting. Warren relaxes his grip on the container and lets go of the lid. He peers through the milky plastic at the object inside.

"What's it doing?" Phthsspitty-snapp says, recoiling a little from the blurry, polyethylene-filtered face filling the video screen.

Jerry shrugs. "Maybe it's thinking." The face recedes and the now-familiar rhythm of the alien's gait resumes. "It's taking the probe back into the shelter," Jerry marvels.

Warren slips into the house, plastic box behind his back. The bathroom door is still closed. He hurries into the study, picking his way between stacks of books and a couple of lawn chairs. As he pauses, looking for a good spot, he hears Penny turn on the hot water for a bath. He sets the Tupperware® down in an empty corner shielded by a pile of field guides and spiral-bound notebooks full of random scribblings, poems, and doodles.

Jerry turns to Phthsspitty-snapp. "Ring up the linguist," he says. "Find out how far the linguistic analysis has progressed."

"Why?" she asks, then says, "I mean, yes sir," when she sees the look on his face.

Warren crouches over the plastic box, shaking his head. The acorn lies motionless, looking as if it will never move—as if it never could have.

"Seventy percent," Phthsspitty-snapp reports.

"Good enough." Jerry reaches down and flicks a buckle-like switch, releasing his front leg from the body seal that holds him to his seat at the probe's control console. He feels for the rear release, finds it, and stands up as it comes undone.

Phthsspitty-snapp stares up at him, mouth open. "What are you doing? The protocols...."

Jerry just says, "Come on," and releases her rear leg for her.

"But our directives...."

He meets her eyes, leaning in a little closer. "Don't you want to see it?" he asks. "I mean, really see it?"

"Umm...."

"Who's going to know?"

She grins, stands up, and follows him through the narrow passage behind their seats.

The first thing Warren notices is a gentle rocking of the probe, almost like a jumping bean starting to wake up. And then the outline of the probe blurs a little, a piece lifting along the top. When did his heart start pounding again? Slowly he peels back the lid of the container and peers in. A little door or hatch has opened near the back end of the acorn. A few pinpricks of light glimmer inside, and then two tiny people climb out.

"Are you sure about this?" Phthsspitty-snapp asks, standing close to Jerry on the fuselage of the probe.

Jerry laughs. "Not at all."

Warren feels as if he has a ridge of stiff bristles on the nape of his neck and no eyelids at all. Then he laughs, not at what he is seeing but at the way a long dream can seem so real. Soon it'll be morning, he thinks. And I'll get up, have a quick shower, and walk out on the levee. I'll see redwing blackbirds, yellow-crowned night herons, mullets jumping, maybe a few turtles poking their heads up for air, and a bunch of water bottles stuck in the weeds. Not a single flying black acorn or miniature person.

"We want the explore this planet," Jerry says, and a microphone on his shoulder transmits his words to the probe, which translates and amplifies them.

Warren laughs again. "Of course you do. And of course you...mostly...speak my language. But why are you so small?"

"I fined that the scale of organisms deepens on the scale of the place around. Will you release us to explore this planet?"

Warren leans in as close as he can. "You're sideways."

Phthsspitty-snapp coughs, and Jerry puts a steadying hand on her back shoulder. It takes a certain fortitude to stand your ground before the broad, slightly oily face of an enormous alien life-form, its pungent breath washing over you, warming the air. "From are punt of few, you are sideways," Jerry replies.

"Otherwise we look almost the same," Warren muses. "Two legs, two arms, one head. Pretty much the same face."

"Yes."

"How many fingers and toes do you have?"

"Hate fingers, ten toes."

Warren holds up his hand, wiggling his fingers. "Ten fingers, ten toes. But maybe you already knew that."

"We noted ten, but your toes are covert."

"How long have you been exploring this planet?"

"We have not started much."

"So when I picked you up this morning, you had just landed? Am I the first person you've seen?"

"Yes."

What do I do with them? Warren wonders, moving a hair closer to get a better look. They are just like little people, with their heads and feet turned to one side as if they are about to sashay. Could they be dangerous? Who knows what alien weaponry or mind-control ability they possess? But then again, wouldn't it be better to keep dangerous aliens trapped in a Tupperware® container than to release them into the world?

"What's it doing?" Phthsspitty-snapp says again, staring up into the hairy nostril of the alien. "Is it going to eat us?"

"Probably not," Jerry says, forgetting that the probe is broadcasting everything he says.

"Are you—?" Warren begins. He stops himself, deciding instead to ask the question silently. *Are you reading my mind?* The little aliens just blink at him. "Why are you exploring this planet?" he asks out loud.

"Together information," Jerry says.

"Why?"

The aliens exchange a micro-glance. "We have interest in come pairing other planets to our one," Jerry says. "We explored many planets."

"Way to dodge the question," Phthsspitty-snapp murmurs. "You should go into politics."

"We can use your help," Jerry adds, extending his front arm toward Warren.

Warren gazes at the aliens and takes a breath to reply. He hears the bathroom door open. "Sorry," he whispers, and hurriedly pushes the lid back onto the container and stands up.

Penny stands in the hallway, holding her nightgown in one hand, the other gripping the top of a towel wrapped around her body. "What are you doing?" she asks, with the inflection of one who comes across grave robbers.

"Just taking care—I mean, this is not the roach." Warren brandishes the Tupperware®, but gingerly. "No, I got rid of the roach. It's that black acorn thing. And you're not going to believe this." He stops, unable to say aloud that he has two aliens the size of pill-bugs in his hand. So he holds up the container and carefully peels back the lid.

"You already showed me that," Penny says. "Did you see it fly again?"

"No, look closer," Warren says, peering into the box. "Where did they go?" He picks up the probe cautiously, feeling for the hatch opening. "Yoo-hoo," he calls.

Penny studies Warren's face. "Where did *what* go?"

"The...uh...the...there were some...flakes that came off this thing. Flakes. I thought they might be a clue, but I guess they blew away or something."

"That's what I wouldn't believe? Some unbelievable flakes?" One hand on hip, one eyebrow raised.

"I don't know why I said that," Warren says. "Why did I say that? Did I really say that?"

Penny narrows her eyes, hesitating. Warren gives her a winning smile, knowing that she is reviewing their whole life together, from the day she approached him in a vacant lot. *You're up to something,* she squints. *But I don't have the energy to find out what it is, and it's probably nothing much.* She shakes her head and moves into the bedroom, shaking out her nightgown.

"Thanks a lot," Warren murmurs to the probe.

Phthsspitty-snapp is grinning at Jerry from her copilot's seat in the probe. "This species appears to mate for life, much like our own," she says, pretending to make notes for the initial report.

"Indeed," Jerry says, but he isn't smiling. He turns down the volume on the probe's PA system. "We are preferring to keep our explorision secret," he says to Warren. "For now."

Warren cradles the Tupperware©®™ container in the crook of his elbow, holding it up high near his face. "How did you get here? How far away is your planet? Did you bring weapons? What kind of exploration is this?" he whispers, hurrying to the kitchen to get out of range of Penny's sharp hearing.

"We are interesting in that species' use of natural resources and weigh of life," Jerry says.

"True enough," Phthsspitty-snapp muses.

Warren sets the container on the breakfast table, leaving it open. He sits down, leaning close. "You sure you didn't come here to enslave us and take over? That's what usually happens in the movies."

"We only coming to explore and analyze."

"Promise?"

"Yes."

If I brought this thing to some kind of scientist at the university, he could analyze it, Warren thinks. Subject it to tests. X-ray it. We could go to the media, hold a press conference. "But why?" he asks. "Why are you exploring and analyzing this planet?"

Jerry mutes the PA. "I thought I already told him why," he says.

"Your answer wasn't very satisfying," Phthsspitty-snapp says.

He hesitates, finger still on the mute button.

"Make it sound dramatic," Phthsspitty-snapp says. "Tell him we need his help. But don't lie."

Jerry nods. "Our own planet is trebled," he tells Warren. "We belief there is much to learn from your weigh of life. Perhaps you will guide us."

Just then Penny calls from the bedroom, and Warren leaves the open container on the breakfast table. "I think I could eat an egg and some toast," she says, sitting on the bed half dressed. When Warren gets back to the kitchen, the black acorn hovers near the window, expectant.

"I'll do what I can," Warren says. "But I've got a life."

"Understood," says the quiet alien voice.

J. Monologue: Oily makes infrequent use of monologue, in which a character delivers speech at length, uninterrupted by other characters. As user of Oily, you accept monologue as a reasonable feature of Oily, refraining from subscribing to the idea, espoused by at least one literary agent who shall remain nameless, that monologue is unrealistic or unconventional, for in certain circumstances individuals do deliver relatively lengthy monologues without interruption, as occurs when the character "Warren" explains his actions in the kitchen as the aliens observe, beginning by saying, "All right, so I'm preparing some food for my wife," and continuing with, "We call the first meal of the day 'breakfast.' This is bread, which is, um, made by grinding up the seeds of a plant called 'wheat,' then mixing the seed powder with water and sugar—which is a plant-based sweetener—and...other stuff...? Well, let's see, it's got yeast, of course, which is a bacterium or microbe or something, which makes bubbles so the seed-powder/water/sugar mixture expands. What else does it have? 'Two percent or less of each of the following....' Salt, which is a mineral we dig up or make from seawater to make food taste good—wait, it's...um...sodium chloride! Okay, and canola oil, which is a liquid fat from some sort of plant; sodium stearyl lactylate, calcium stearoyl-2-lactylate, monoglycerides, calcium iodate, ethoxylated mono and diglycerides, calcium peroxide, azodicarbonamide, calcium sulfate, monocalcium phosphate, and soy lecithin. Most of those are chemicals, except for the lecithin, which is maybe a plant-based gummy substance. I'm not sure what those chemicals are or how they are made. So the bread goes in this thing, which we call a 'toaster,' which uses electricity to heat up metal wires to make the bread crisp, but we also eat bread plain without toasting it. Now I'm getting a pan out of this cabinet and putting it on the stove and turning it on. Electricity heats up these coils, which heats up the pan. This is butter, which is salted fat from the milk of these big animals we call 'cows,' and we use it for cooking so stuff won't stick to the pan, although this is a non-stick pan so I don't really have to use butter, but it'll make the egg taste better. So I'm getting an egg out of the refrigerator, which is this big white box here that somehow uses electricity to keep food cold so that it won't spoil as quickly. This is an egg from a chicken, which is a bird about yea big that we eat the meat of and also the eggs, which we cook all sorts of ways and put in cakes, which are sort of like bread but much sweeter. See? I crack it, put the gooey insides in the pan, which is pretty hot by now, and it starts cooking. This white powder is salt, which I told you about earlier, and this black powder is pepper, which is another kind of seed powder, but we don't make bread from it—that would be bizarre and nasty—but it makes things taste a little spicier. Ooh, the toast just popped up. See how it's kind of crunchy now? So I'm putting some butter on it."

K. Arc: The conventions of narrative dictate that the story contained within Oily follow a loose structural pattern consisting of rising action, climax, and denouement. The creator of Oily has adhered to these conventions. As a result, Oily begins with the protagonist encountering a problem (i.e., the mystery of the "black acorn"), just as the tale of Cinderella begins with its protagonist encountering a problem (i.e., loss of parents). Actions that occur as the narrative continues cause an increase ("rise") in the complexity and repercussions of the problem, e.g. the aliens emerge from the probe or the step-family enslaves Cinderella. The narrative "takes off" (i.e., the action begins to rise more steeply) as the result of a significant complication near the beginning of the narrative (e.g., the king declares that all eligible maidens are to attend a ball, or the aliens make a shocking declaration). Please note that quite a number of dialogues and actions occur before the shocking declaration. Jerry first asks Warren in his kitchen, after Warren delivers a monologue, "May we take samples?" and Warren subsequently says, "What, of the toast? Sure, there's plenty to go around and you're not very big. Oh, you're touching the toast. I guess your little spaceship is probably pretty clean. Careful, that's hot, but I guess you have sensors and all to tell you that. You're touching everything, I guess," at which point Jerry remarks that, "This pan has a polymer coating," and Warren says, "That's right. Teflon™. I guess it's some kind of plastic," and the exchange of dialogue continues with Jerry asking, "And how is the electricity who powers the 'toaster' and 'stove' generated?"

As user of Oily, you understand the need for patience as the story unfolds; the creator of Oily understands his obligation to provide an entertaining unfolding of the story by including plot complications and/or potential plot complications. These conventions are deeply ingrained in our psyches, so much so that as readers most of us are not aware of our expectations that action rise, that once the climax is reached the story must end quickly, etc. Which is not to say that there are no narrative works of art that break and/or flout these conventions, but they do so with an awareness of those conventions, of how each breaking or flout-ation affects readers who subscribe, wittingly or unwittingly, to such conventions. Giving a story the right shape is a sophisticated skill, not easily learned, and sometimes a writer has to reshape a whole book to give it the right shape, and sometimes the reshaping process takes a few years because first the writer has to get to the point where he or she can clearly see the story he or she has written, which is as difficult as making a map of a forest by wandering around among its trees. A writer reads and re-reads, sometimes waiting months between readings with the hope that the passage of time will provide the necessary perspective, the proper elevation from which to view the lay of the land. A writer asks others to read the manuscript, others who can the see forest for the trees. It's a little like sending a friend to the top of an observation tower and then trying to improve your map of the forest based on what your friend tells you when your friend returns to ground level. Having done such things, the creator of Oily understands the need for complications, viz.:

"And how is the elect trickery which pars the 'toaster' and 'stove' generated?"

"Well, it comes to the house through wires. See out there? Those black wires carry electricity to all of the houses. They come from power plants, which make loads of electricity and send it out all over the city. I guess a lot of them use coal, but some use oil or nuclear power. A few even use hydroelectric or wind power." Warren watches the acorn float here and there, from the stove to the floor to the counter to the newspaper to the pantry door and the ceiling, dipping briefly down to each like a dragonfly laying eggs on a pond.

"A variety of materials," Jerry remarks to Phthsspitty-snapp, forgetting to press MUTE.

"Right," Warren says. "The floor is ceramic tiles, which are made by baking special muds called clay. All of these cabinets are wood, which comes from huge plants like those outside the window. They're called 'trees.' A lot of metal in here, mostly steel I guess, which we make with iron that we dig up out of the ground and mix with some other metals so it won't rust. Oxidize? That's paper, which is made by grinding up trees with water and chemicals and then drying it in thin sheets, and so are those. The countertop is plastic. So are these knobs, the refrigerator handles, that container, that cup, the toaster handles. Lots of stuff. The walls are, well, wallboard, which is made of...I'm not sure what it's made of."

"A soft mineral encased in thick 'paper' and covered with an artificial coating," Jerry says.

"Really? I guess that's right. Drywall has paper on it, and I guess the plastery stuff inside is made of minerals."

Phthsspitty-snapp can tell that Jerry is getting annoyed. He pays little attention to what the alien is saying, focusing more on the readings provided by the sampling lance.

When Warren brings Penny her tea, toast, and egg, she asks him if he has had the radio on in the kitchen. "The radio?" he says. "Oh, right—talking. Yes. Talk radio. NPR®."

[POTENTIAL COMPLICATION]

"Someone on there sounds just like you," she says, eyeing him. He turns to the closet and busies himself with changing uniforms, shedding the shorts and tee shirt of an early-morning levee walker and donning the khakis and oxford of a community-college English instructor. The whole time he worries that the black acorn will float past in the hall, and what will Penny with her glasses on think? He also *hopes* that the black acorn will float past in the hall, because then Penny will believe what he has told her.

Jerry and Phthsspitty-snapp cruise around the kitchen, sampling thermoplastic and thermoset polymers—Tupperware™ containers, toaster handles, stove knobs, countertop, garbage bag, knife handles, spatula, light switch, light fixture, scrubber, soap dish, detergent bottle. The list of materials on the display screen lengthens rapidly: ethylenes, propylenes, styrenes, phenolics, polyurethanes, and polyvinyl chloride. "I'm going to test the tensile strength of this transparent silica," Jerry murmurs, maneuvering close to the window.

"Wait," Phthsspitty-snapp says.

"We've waited long enough. The protocols say nothing about gathering information from resident species."

"They do say not to antagonize them," she points out. "By breaking a window, for example."

[POTENTIAL COMPLICATION]

"We've got a report due," Jerry says. But he backs the probe away from the window, fuming. Instead, he steers it out into the hallway, careful to stay near the ceiling, and goes around the corner to the study to sample CD cases, ink cartridges, various parts of a laptop, ballpoint pens, a lampshade, a spiral-bound notebook, letter trays, the arms of a desk chair, a digital camera, and the packaging of a new flash key.

"Okay," Warren says loudly as he leaves the bedroom. "I'll be going now. I'll lock the door when I leave. I'm going to work now...." He looks for the flying acorn, determined not to leave it in the house alone with Penny. He finds it hovering expectantly by the front door.

"We'll follow the transmission lines to a power plant," Jerry says to Phthsspitty-snapp.

"You never took anthropology, did you?" she asks. "I guess in your day the emphasis was on hard science."

"What's that got to do with anything?"

"Look, this thing might not know the exact composition of the walls of his shelter, but he can provide lots of structural information. How long would it have taken us to figure out that their power plants burn hydrocarbons or use nuclear fission or hydroelectric power? We can verify what he said, but we don't have to find it out for ourselves."

"I don't want to be stuck following this guy around one tiny corner of the planet," Jerry says, nevertheless piloting the probe through the grass near Warren's feet as he walks to his car. "But we'll try it your way for a little while."

Maybe they think I'm a god, Warren thinks. They did stand there very respectfully, looking up at me with their little narrow faces. Some global crisis grips their tiny planet, and they have come to me for help, detecting my exceptional ability with some sort of subtle technology. Monster alien insects might be preying on them, and they'll teleport me to their solar system to do battle. Or they've run out of trees or clay or farmland and wish to adopt Earth's technology. Either way, they'll build statues of me in their teeming cities. What a strange dream. "This is a car," he says helpfully. "We use it to transport ourselves to various destinations, such as schools and stores, which are...well, maybe you have schools and stores on your planet?" The aliens do not answer, and so Warren pushes on. "Anyway. This metal thing is a key, which unlocks the doors and starts the engine. Each house has a driveway like this for parking cars. See that metal box on that pole? It's a mailbox, and every house has one. Every day—well, almost—a government employee brings paper communications from corporations, friends, family members, and so on, and puts them in the mailbox. All right. Here we go. I'm going to turn here. There goes another car. Across there is City Park. I don't know if you have parks, but they're large—well, some are small—areas of cleared or forested land, or even paved land, where we can engage in outdoor activities or just relax."

"What motivates this vehicle?" the acorn asks.

"Motivates? It's not...it doesn't—I'm controlling it. See? When I rotate the steering wheel, the front wheels turn to the right or left, and I've got pedals down here—."

Jerry interrupts the alien. "Excuse me, no—."

"Seventy percent," Phthsspitty-snapp whispers.

Jerry nods. "How is it propelled?"

"Ah, I see. There's an internal combustion engine up there, with pistons and...a crankshaft? That turns gears that turn the wheels? In this car, it's the front wheels. It's metal, by the way. The whole outside of the car is painted steel and the engine is aluminum, I think, or steel and aluminum, maybe a little copper here and there—well, the wires are copper, at least...."

"And what is the fool of the engine?"

"Ah. Gasoline."

The probe floats here and there, clicking, while Warren drives and natters on about a railroad bridge and various street signs. Inside, the list of polymers grows still longer as Jerry samples upholstery, door handles, dashboard, radio. "I've seen enough," he tells Phthsspitty-snapp. "It's pretty clear what's going on here." He pulls up Scanomatrix 2.9, a software program that utilizes input from various sensors to find escape routes for captive probes.

"Give it a chance," Phthsspitty-snapp says. "It might not be as bad as Botruntun."

Jerry stares hard at the Scanomatrix 2.9 interface. "You heard about that, huh?"

"Of course I heard about it. Everybody heard about it."

[COMPLICATION]

"And you knew it was me?"

"Not at the time. But do you think the Exploratory Board would keep that a secret from a young intern assigned to your mission?"

"What exactly did they say?"

"Just that you were the project leader on Botruntun and had been found to be 64.32% responsible for what happened."

"And so you just assumed I was some kind of hothead."

"Maybe. Until I met you."

"I don't suppose they gave you my side of the story."

"No, but I had a feeling you had a side, and I didn't trust the rumors."

"What rumors? That I fell in love with an alien?"

"Yep. Those rumors. Didn't believe those rumors. Nope."

Jerry smiles, wagging his head. "That's always the rumor. People have no imagination. Or too much, if they think a Xxzzrrrvan could fall in love with an amphibious reptile four times our size."

"There was that clip of you saying the Botruntions were beautiful—"

"I said they were a *beautiful species.* Watching them interact was like being at the opera. The seven prehensile tails, the musical language, the constant ritual dances...."

"What's it doing?" The vehicle has stopped.

"Sometimes I come out here before work," the alien is saying, unbuckling from some sort of restraint harness. "I thought you might want to see it." Turning the probe this way and that and studying the video display, Jerry can see that the vehicle is just off the road, facing a flat expanse of short green plants just like the ones surrounding the alien house. The alien opens the vehicle door and stands up, holding the door for the probe. Jerry pilots it through. He sees no other aliens in the wide space in front of them, so as the alien begins to walk, Jerry keeps the probe in an inconspicuous position near the alien's hip.

"Ooh, locomotion scan," Phthsspitty-snapp says, reaching for an auxiliary display. "It's weird how they walk sideways." She watches what she can see of the giant alien's torso, hip, and upper leg, noting the complex gait that makes them grind and jostle.

Jerry notes the approach of a hill or low ridge that runs straight to the left and right, perhaps twelve feet high, carpeted with green flora. As the alien climbs the hill, recognition dawns upon Jerry. "This is about where we landed," he says, and pulls up the historical map for confirmation. The wandering blue line tracing their recent movements makes a loop, and the loop is tiny. Jerry sighs and widens the zoom on the map until he can see that the loop is just a speck at the edge of one of the planet's several continents.

Warren sits down halfway between the top of the levee and the edge of the canal. The probe hesitates beside him, then sinks down into the grass and slides toward the water's edge. It does its dragonfly thing, dipping and clicking against an old water bottle, a Ziploc™ bag, a Styrofoam™ cup, a grocery bag half submerged in mud.

"So careless," Jerry says angrily. "Just leaving it lying around everywhere."

"I want to ask it some questions," Phthsspitty-snapp says.

"And their vehicles are enormous. We need a sample of their fuel." He plunges the probe into the brownish water, and the video display shows the back end of a turtle fleeing into the murk. The bottom is soft smooth mud, interrupted here and there by sodden sticks and slimy metal cans. The water deepens a little in the middle of the canal, and there is just enough light to make out the fuzzy shape of an old wheel like the ones on the alien's vehicle, fuzzy with algae. "Damn it," Jerry says, and guns the probe's propulsion system.

Warren sits wondering how long the probe can stay underwater, then gets distracted by a pair of least terns flying past over the canal, studying the surface. The sounds of traffic recede, and he notes the call of a kingfisher somewhere across the water. A mullet leaps from the water to his left, then leaps again a few yards further along. Sure doesn't feel like a dream right now, he thinks, digging his fingers into the grass. The mullet pops up again, only this time it isn't a mullet but a long black acorn, and it zooms off toward the pumping station at the end of the canal. He wishes Penny were there with him, laughing at the mullet and expressing her affection for terns. If Penny were well, if she were still the Penny who wore a purple dress and kicked at the sand, she would be here, too.

Phthsspitty-snapp knows not to say anything as Jerry guides the probe at top speed over the ruffled surface of the water. She holds her breath at the sudden approach of a large ceramic bridge, holds on as the probe banks to the left and rises steeply. It lurches to a stop over the bridge. She and Jerry stare at the video screen, both of them grim. Two rivers of vehicles flow beneath them, one in each direction. Some of the vehicles are ten times the size of the one the alien drove, and they move three abreast. Jerry dials up some zoom and can't find the end of the road in either direction. He orders an air sample. Before the results can scroll up on the display, he whips the probe around and aims it at the colorful dot on the levee grass half a mile away. "Don't," Phthsspitty-snapp gasps, even as the dot blows up until the side of Warren's head fills the screen.

Warren hears a rush of air and turns to find the black acorn hovering just off his left shoulder. "Where'd you go?" he asks.

"Ask your questions," Jerry tells Phthsspitty-snapp.

She speaks into the dash-mounted microphone, leaning closer to it than necessary. "Hello alien," she says. "This is Special Assistant Phthsspitty-snapp Johnson...speaking. I am a special assistant to Head Researcher Jerry Boberry."

"Okay," Warren says.

"Get on with it," Jerry says. "It sounds the same no matter who's speaking."

"Right." She nods. "We would like to request certain information of you."

"You sound like a robot," Jerry says. "Just speak naturally."

"How many of your species inhabit this planet?" Phthsspitty-snapp asks.

"Let's see." Warren looks thoughtfully up into the sky. "I think we're up to about seven billion."

"Damn," Jerry says.

Phthsspitty-snapp clears her throat. "And how many vehicles such as yours?"

"Gosh, at least a billion, I'm guessing. Two billion?"

"And does each vehicle burn gasoline?"

"Most of them do. A good many use diesel."

"Please recite the chemical composition of gasoline and diesel, including any additives."

"Huh?"

"Move aside." Jerry lets loose an exasperated sigh. "How are the gasoline and diesel fuels created?"

"I don't know exactly. They come from oil."

"What kind of oil?"

"Petroleum."

"Where does the petroleum come from?"

"Underground."

For a moment nothing happens. Warren watches the probe as it hovers off his left shoulder. Phthsspitty-snapp holds her breath, sneaking glances at Jerry, who sits motionless, staring at the alien's broad face. Finally he looks down, flicks his fingers here and there across the console, and says one last thing: "Your foolish species is doomed."

[SHOCKING DECLARATION]

With a faint whoosh the black acorn shoots into the sky as if jerked on a string and disappears. Warren looks up into the blank blue above him. "What did you say?" he calls. "I didn't catch that last thing you said."

Following the above shocking declaration, users of the text of Oily should expect an increase in the angle at which the action in the narrative rises, just as the angle at which the action rises increases after Cinderella's king announces plans for a singles' ball.

L. Exposition: The process by which fictional texts such as Oily deliver contextual information is known as "exposition." As a reader of fiction, you understand that Oily's exposition may be gradual, oblique, delayed, and/or partial. You also understand and accept that fictional exposition is connotative rather than denotative. You understand the advantages of such exposition over bald, explicit exposition, i.e. you have no desire to read a fictional text which begins: "Warren, a 34 year old, five foot ten college writing instructor, unlocked the side door of his 1400-square-foot New Orleans house on a spring day and shouted excitedly to his sick wife, 'Penny, you've got to see this!' In his hand he held an oblong black object that looked like an acorn. It was actually an alien probe, and there were two tiny aliens named Jerry and Phthsspitty-snapp inside it, and they had come to Earth in order to...."

THE PRECEDING EXCERPT IS HYPOTHETICAL AND BY NO MEANS A PART OF THE ACTUAL TEXT OF OILY. ITS BASIS ON THE ACTUAL TEXT OF OILY IS INTENDED ONLY TO PROVIDE A DEMONSTRATION VIA CONTRAST. IT IS INTENDED ONLY FOR THE PRIVATE USE OF OUR AUDIENCE.

Readers anxious to learn more about the fictitious history of the planet Xxzzrrrva are advised to practice patience (see Article V.B) and pay attention to the following excerpt, in which exposition has been italicized.

THE FOLLOWING EXCERPT IS ACTUAL BUT HAS BEEN MODIFIED TO ACCENTUATE EXPOSITION. USERS WHO PURLOIN, STEAL, OR OTHERWISE APPROPRIATE THE FOLLOWING OR ANY OTHER EXCERPT FOR THEIR OWN USE ARE SUBJECT TO LITIGATION BY THE CREATOR OF OILY, WHO HAS INCONTROVERTIBLE PROOF THAT HE AND HE ALONE HAS BEEN THE CREATOR, ORIGINATOR, AND AUTHOR OF OILY.

"Slow down," Phthsspitty-snapp manages to say, jaw clenched tight against the oppressive force of acceleration.

Jerry laughs bitterly. "Slow down! You've read the reports, right? *The last Xxzzrrrvan analysis found perfect conditions—warm temperatures, plentiful water, giant forests, no sign of sentient life.* And look now!" He does slow down, finally, leveling the probe near a layer of high thin clouds and making a slow turn. The ragged coastline where they landed and Warren wheels across the display.

"*A lot can happen in a hundred million years,*" Phthsspitty-snapp suggests.

"Yeah, and fast." Jerry fiddles with the controls. "Ceramics," he says, and the display shows a thick weave of black lines between tangled cities. "Electromagnetic" makes an overlay of knotted yellow fabric appear. "Metallic" adds pink clusters.

"*Maybe the Board shouldn't have interfered,*" Phthsspitty-snapp says.

"*Xxzzrrrva is in the business of interfering,*" Jerry says. "What was it again?" he asks, knowing by now that Phthsspitty-snapp will recall the details. She is a grad student, after all.

"Reptilians. Diverse species of all sizes and configurations, from tiny vegetarians to carnivores the size of mountains. Most with brains smaller than their eyeballs, but *evolutionary analysis raised the slight possibility of sentient development.*"

"*And so we just stepped in, formulated a potion, and wiped them out, opening the door for these giant humanoids.*" Jerry waves at the planet below.

"That's one way to put it."

He leans closer to the display. "Look at the sea," he says. Phthsspitty-snapp reaches out to adjust the zoom, and Jerry sits back. "Are those islands?" He flicks off the overlays and the islands disappear. He brings them back. They are mostly pink and yellow, and they come in different sizes.

"Mostly on the continental shelf," Phthsspitty-snapp murmurs, looking at where the dots are most thickly crowded. "Offshore housing?"

"But why? There's all that space between cities."

Phthsspitty-snapp shrugs, hitting a toggle switch. "There are over four thousand of them, whatever they are."

Jerry just shakes his head and grasps the flight controls. Phthsspitty-snapp stiffens as the probe dives sharply, accelerating hard. One of the bigger islands grows quickly, filling the video screen as the probe descends. Phthsspitty-snapp manages to clear the overlays and return to normal zoom before Jerry levels off the probe just above the wrinkled sea. He stops, pointing the probe squarely at an enormous contraption that was a pink and yellow dot a few moments before. It has four stout legs supporting a gangly mishmash of pods and platforms and skeletal metallic limbs. A giant plume of flame roars out of a long tube extending over the water. "It looks like an antique," Phthsspitty-snapp says.

"It looks like an artifact." Jerry slides the probe to one side, keeping it pointed at the contraption.

"What's it for?" she asks.

"You really don't know? What's the worst thing it could be for?"

"Shooting down Xxzzrrrvan mother ships?"

"Don't you see the central conduit extending toward the seafloor?"

"Central conduit? Now who's been watching too much sci-fi? You mean that big pipe?"

"Yes, that big pipe. What do you suppose it's for?" Without waiting for her answer, Jerry drives the probe at top speed toward the contraption, whose clanking, beeping, roaring symphony becomes deafening. In a blink the probe stops hard to hover just over the heads of a team of earthlings in white helmets and blue jumpsuits, the four of them running here and there, shouting at one another, around a stout spinning pipe covered in black goo. None of them notice a long black acorn hovering above them, gliding here and there for a few minutes before striking the drill pipe a glancing blow and speeding off over the water, disappearing into the distance.

"Pretty high sulfur content," Phthsspitty-snapp remarks. Jerry is busy exceeding the Exploratory Board's planetary speed limit, dodging fishing boats and cargo ships. He cuts the throttle, squeezing to a halt before a lonely ceramic rectangle bristling with rusting metal pipes and valve wheels. "Probably 3,000 are this size," Jerry says. "Idiots. They're doomed."

"Maybe it's only this region," Phthsspitty-snapp says.

"Oh, you mean the rest of the planet is populated by another species, which rides livestock and builds fires? Or maybe earthlings on other continents are more advanced and have discovered other ways to illuminate their cities and power their vehicles? Or maybe most earthlings have no interest in illumination and smoke-belching vehicles and disposable polymers because they are more spiritual and intellectual?" He shakes his head dismissively.

"Well, why not?"

"It never works that way."

"Stranger things have happened."

"Stranger...? *You mean like the time we found a planet ruled by benevolent robots pampering the species that created them? Or the time we found a planet ruled by malicious robots using the species that had created them as energy sources? Or maybe you mean that dismal little planet crowded with sophisticated cannibalistic microbes? Or the one with just two species, one plant and one animal? The arsenic-based crustaceans living on a planet too close to its sun to support life?*

The rock-eating invertebrates under the ice of a planet too far from its sun to support life?"

"Well, why not?"

Jerry points the probe skyward and punches it back to full speed. Within moments they are high enough to see the whole green and brown continent spread out below them. He reapplies the overlays that highlight ceramic, metallic, and electromagnetic structures. "You see where we were?" he asks. "That medium-sized city near that almost circular sea? Look at the megalopolis to the west! You want to see more?" He points the probe toward the darkening east and speeds over the circular sea and then a broad ocean. Within a few minutes, two other continents appear in the distance, the land invisible but the lights of cities shining and the overlays showing the same thick clusters and tangled lines of civilization. "Satisfied?" Jerry sneers.

V. USER RESPONSIBILITIES

A. Suspension of Disbelief: As user of Oily you accept a responsibility to willingly suspend your tendency, however strong and/or weak, to reject the possibility that life exists on other planets and that interstellar travel is feasible. Access your inner Carl Sagan. In addition, you willingly and knowingly ignore all explicit and/or implicit evidence ruling out the existence of a narrator who could report upon the (sometimes simultaneous) actions, words, and thoughts of various human and non-human persons in a variety of locations, including but not limited to the interiors of houses and/or vehicles (including "space ships") in various distant terrestrial and extra-terrestrial locales. Should the narrative suddenly shift to the Xxzzrrrvan mother ship and to previously unknown characters named Hmmm and

Gravy, you do promise and solemnly swear to play along, perhaps even feeling your interest piqued by their sudden introduction, which begins with Gravy, sitting at the control console on the bridge of the mother ship, turning briefly at the sound of the door sliding open with a brisk whoosh, Star Trek™ style. Hmmm enters, holding high his carefully arranged head of gray hair. Without invitation, he crosses the bridge and stands behind Gravy, eyes scanning the vast console as if he knew the significance of every diode and rheostat. "At ease," he says. Gravy, already at ease and under no obligation to be otherwise, flashes a wry grin and adjusts a stabilizer. "All systems go?" Hmmm asks after a moment.

"All systems go," Gravy says, doing his best to suppress an eye roll.

"Very good," Hmmm says. "And tell me, how closely have you been tracking the probe?"

"Periodic communications," Gravy says. "And of course every sensor is closely monitored."

"Yes of course. And what are they doing now?"

"What are they doing now?"

"Yes. Or...what have they done thus far?"

"Thus far?"

"Yes, Captain Gravy. Thus far."

"They made landfall less than seven znorbiks ago." Gravy twists a dial and a map appears on a small display on the left end of the console. He points to it, and Hmmm leans down, squinting.

"They've hardly moved!" Hmmm declares, frowning. "They've just stayed within a small area at the edge of this continent." He pokes a finger at the diagram and glares at Gravy, who shrugs. "Call them up!"

"Call them up?"

"Yes." Hmmm waves at the console. "Patch me through to Jerry."

"My communications officer went down to the snack bar," Gravy says. "As soon as he gets back—"

"Very well." Hmmm squints at the map again. "Now they're moving. Crossing the ocean to the east. Can they hear me?" He bends closer to the console and raises his voice. "Jerry? I want you to scan the polar regions next. Can you hear me?"

Gravy watches Hmmm, one eyebrow raised. "They can't hear you," he says.

"Of course not." Hmmm straightens, clears his throat, and scans the broad console again. "Captain," he says quietly, sidling closer. "I wonder if there's any way to hack into their video feed. Maybe your communications officer could rig something up."

"Sure thing," Gravy whispers, winking. He taps the console and points to a seat on the far end of the bridge, where a small display has flickered to life.

"Ah, very good," Hmmm murmurs, and practically tiptoes his way over to the seat.

B. Patience: Although the creator of Oily understands that users of Oily may spend more time watching movies and television than they spend reading, users must understand and accept that the enjoyment of Oily may at times require patience. Various narrative threads diverge over the course of the novel, which necessitates alternation between multiple settings and event sequences. Imagine a child conducting a race between three toy horses by advancing first one, then the other, and then the third (perhaps the child has one arm in a sling as the result of a playground injury and thus cannot advance two horses at once). In this hypothetical scenario, the black horse represents Jerry and Phthsspitty-snapp in their probe high above the dark eastern Atlantic; the brown horse represents Gravy and Hmmm orbiting Earth in the Xxzzrrrvan mother ship; and the white horse represents Warren and Penny on the ground in New Orleans, where Warren has just been wondering how to explain to his students that tiny aliens have made him late—just five minutes or so, but that's ten percent of the class session, and he knows that if he doesn't get there in another two minutes they'll start leaving. He wonders whether he should set his plans aside and sit/lean on his desk, clasping his hands and holding the students spellbound with the news that sideways little humanoids wander the universe, visiting planets. Or perhaps he should just rush in and plunge into the day's activities, struggle to cram them into the next forty minutes, after which the class will pack up with a chorus of zipping and Velcro™-tearing so that they can spend the last few minutes staring impatiently at the clock on the wall. "Watch for UFOs," he jokes as he dismisses them, but the students just roll their eyes and bustle through the door.

"Where have you been?" Penny asks when he finally gets home. She sits on the side of the bed, hands on the edge, head bent.

Warren just shoves the closet door aside. "You want that green skirt?"

"Red herring," she says, and Warren freezes. Dead to rights, he thinks. She probably already knows that he went a little out of his way after class, stopping at the levee to look at the water, although she couldn't know that he walked to the spot where he last saw the black acorn to scan the horizon, move around conspicuously, and wait as long as he could before jogging to the car and rushing home. She coughs and starts over. "That red herringbone dress. The one with the black buttons."

Half an hour later Warren holds the glass door for her and they walk into Dr. Raversonville's office. Warren strides to the receptionist's desk while Penny shuffles to a pink vinyl chair in the waiting area. When he turns to join her after signing in and collecting a clipboard from the receptionist, he feels a jolt of recognition and confusion, because there's Penny, sitting slightly hunched in the chair, not quite leaning back and not quite leaning forward but holding herself just so, hair dull and lips dry. He hasn't seen her from a distance in weeks, and he sees how her malady has changed her, how it forces her body into this crouched pose, not letting her relax and just be there. He feels bad for sometimes wondering if it is all in her head and for feeling impatient as she moved slowly from the house to the Volkswagen and from the Volkswagen to the clinic.

They put their heads together over the clipboard to fill out New Patient Info. The first page is laborious, all names, addresses, phone numbers, and insurance information. The second page is a simple matter of checking the "no" boxes by asthma, COPD, appendicitis, high blood pressure, spinal injury, concussion, amputation, checking the "yes" boxes by dizziness, joint pain, nausea, rash, and writing "none" under Allergies. On page three they let Dr. Raversonville know that Penny does not smoke or drink, has never had a baby, is sexually active (technically) but not HIV-positive, and ingests seven various pain, anti-nausea, anti-migraine, and hormone medications on a daily basis. The next eight pages provide the details of the office's privacy policies in 6-point font. Penny signs it, assuming that by doing so she does not authorize the release of her medical records to the CIA, FBI, KGB, or Interpol.

A half hour later they watch Dr. Raversonville breeze into the examination room, all confident and face-lifty. "Ralph Raversonville," he says, offering each of them a well-practiced handshake, then sits down on a low stool and opens Penny's chart. "So you're a 34-year-old female, don't smoke or drink, BP's a little elevated. Aches and pains, nausea, fatigue, random skin rashes...? How long has this been going on?" He rolls forward to grasp Penny's face with both hands, looking into her eyes and massaging her under the jaw and along her neck.

"Almost a year," Penny says.

"And you've been to a few doctors," he says, rolling away. "And what have they told you?"

"Dr. Crowton thought it might be lupus, but Dr. Moreham ruled that out and said it could be MS. I took MS meds for a while, but she took me off those after a few months. A friend recommended Dr. Cloffermort, and he thought it was chronic fatigue, but Dr. Sofachair decided it was fibromyalgia."

Dr. Raversonville keeps nodding, jotting notes. "And your blood work...?" He flips through a few pages. "Iron a little low last October, otherwise good...."

"Don't forget Dr. Sorely," Warren says. "He thought it was yeast."

"Get out much?" Dr. Raversonville asks, still jotting.

"No."

"Exercise at all?"

"Not any more."

"Right." One more jot, then he looks up, gives them both a reassuring smile. "I can tell you what's wrong."

Penny and Warren speak in unison. "Really?" Both of them know by now that the other would caution against false hope—they have had the conversation enough times that they no longer need to talk about it on the way to the next doctor. But other doctors have been more well-there's-a-chance-it-could-be-this than I-can-tell-you-what's-wrong. And so they lean forward, expectant.

"Sure. I've seen it before." He pulls out a smart phone and starts fiddling with it. "Let me call this in while we talk. Which pharmacy do you use?"

> The hypothetical white horse of Warren and Penny has advanced far enough, and patient users of Oily understand that the narrative will return to Warren and Penny the same way the hypothetical child's hand returns to the hypothetical white horse after first advancing one of the other toy horses, in this case the black horse of Jerry and Phthsspitty-snapp, who still hover high above the darkened eastern Atlantic, gazing down upon the dense net of city lights over the subcontinent we call Europe. Phthsspitty-snapp eyes faint offshore glimmers to the northeast. "It could be that they only have the technology to extract from undersea reservoirs," she says slowly.

"Unlikely," Jerry says. "I thought you studied all of this. That's one of the problems with the curriculum these days, though—they focus on the exceptions, the handful of fluky planets among thousands of predictable cases. What, is that more entertaining or something? Look, a planet bearing sentient life is a fluke. Advanced sentient life is a fluke among flukes. Advanced sentient life that doesn't conform to universal norms is a...super-fluke. The story here is the same as it has been everywhere else. Eventually a species figures out that the black goo lying in puddles in out of the way places is somehow useful, maybe for waterproofing or as fuel for illuminators. Then they figure out that there's more black goo underground near those rare puddles. They find more uses for it, usually as fuel for machines of some kind. Sometimes this all happens slowly, sometimes fast. They find better ways of getting it up out of the ground. Someone figures out how to make things out of the stuff that's left over after you separate out the fuel. Before you know it, a beautiful planet is choking on smoke and litter. It's happening here, and it happened millions of years ago on Xxzzrrrva."

"You should have been a guest speaker at the institute," Phthsspitty-snapp says.

"Very funny."

"No, I'm serious. No one ever gave us the big picture. We kept our heads down in the details and research results and theory."

"The big picture is huge," Jerry says. "And ugly." He snaps the probe into a steep dive toward a cluster of dots just off the coast of the big continent to the south. "Especially when you get up close."

Night vision reveals a coastal bulge of low-lying forest laced with rivers and creeks. It blossoms on the screen and they're flying through trees, dodging the larger limbs, amputating twigs and leaves. The probe bursts into a clearing, giving them a quick glimpse of small shelters, much rougher than the one they visited earlier. In a blink the clearing is gone, but Jerry stops and doubles back. He pauses at the edge of the clearing and maneuvers the probe into a good view of the village. A few aliens sit motionless near a small fire, but otherwise no one is out. "What do you notice?" Jerry asks.

"The shelter roofs are some sort of rough plant fiber," Phthsspitty-snapp says.

"And?"

"I don't see any ceramic roadways."

"What else?"

A furry quadruped trots out from between two shelters and heads toward the fire. It lies down beside one of the aliens, who touches it lightly with one hand. "A companion species!" Phthsspitty-snapp says. "Symbiosis."

"Interesting. Also no illuminators." He pulls up the electromagnetic overlay. Nothing.

Jerry guides the probe through a tight U-turn and takes it up and forward through the forest. Soon they are above the trees, and their next target looms up just to the east: three towering columns of metal shooting huge blooms of fire into the night. Drawing closer, they see a vast geometric clearing beside a wide river and a profusion of pipes, valves, tanks, stout towers, and squat ceramic and metallic buildings. Bright lights blaze all over. The three giant flames bathe the whole complex and the surrounding forest in an orange glow. "Primitive," Jerry murmurs, then hits the go button and the probe shoots forward. It veers north and flies just above the river's surface. A spindly dark shape grows on the screen and the probe dives under water, passing just under the hull of a poorly painted wooden vessel. "Take water samples," Jerry says, and Phthsspitty-snapp massages a control orb.

"Do you think—" she begins.

"Wait!" Jerry says, holding up one hand. He guides the speeding probe back to the surface and takes it high above the river. "Metallic," he says, and studies the landscape below, finally locating a thin black line through the forest to the south. He dives for it and in a moment the probe flies through a long, skinny clearing, almost skimming the surface of a large rusting tube. It goes on for miles, and Jerry is just leaving it for the sky above when they come upon a group of five or six aliens gathered around the tube, some with handheld illuminators. The probe passes dangerously close to one of the aliens, and by the time Jerry has slowed and turned the probe to get a look at them, the group has scattered into the woods, leaving heavy tools on the ground. He drops the probe down and finds a shiny circular depression in the rust, the size of a Xxzzrrrvan hula hoop or an American nickel. It is still warm from the friction of a drill.

Jerry swears, punches a button, and the probe returns to the sky. They fly on and find the place where many smaller tubes join the large tube in clusters of three or four, and they trace one of the clusters to a point where one tube branches off and runs through the jungle to a device similar to the ones on the smaller dots in the Gulf of Mexico.

Phthsspitty-snapp stays quiet, deferring to Jerry's fierce concentration. He shoots the probe back out to the coast and flies out to sea until he locates a gigantic metal boat chugging through the waves, full to the brim with raw petroleum. He quickly programs the sensors to highlight underground metallic structures and soon finds vast constellations of oil rigs in a desert far to the east. They travel high above the planet for Xxzzrrrvan hours, finding petroleum extraction activity in snowy northern regions and along various continental shelves, visiting endless cities ten times the size of that first one, seeing roadways that go on forever and carry thick rivers of vehicles the size of Xxzzrrrvan office buildings and shopping malls. At the end, the probe hovers silently miles above the house of the helpful alien who caught them in a polyethylene container. Jerry looks pained, as if hours of glowering and frowning has given him a headache. "Your thoughts?" he says, through clenched teeth.

"Well," Phthsspitty-snapp begins, "This species is clearly in the early stages of petroleum dependence. The planet is small, but richly stocked with oil, thanks to optimal conditions and, of course, Xxzzrrrvan life-seeding millions of years ago."

"Obviously," Jerry says. "Skip to the recommendation."

"Right. Well, I think we could make a case for simply limiting reproduction...."

"Pah! They've got...let's see." He fiddles with a control orb until a report from the mother ship scrolls into view on the display. "Our little alien pal and his seven billion friends have got about 800,000 active wells. They're pulling about 3 billion gallons of petroleum out of the ground every day."

"Every Xxzzrrrvan day?"

"No, every short little Grawgraw-3 day."

"And what's a gallon?" she asks.

"It's the equivalent of about five hundred oobalings."

"Yikes." Phthsspitty-snapp pauses, gathering her thoughts. "Nevertheless," she continues. "The majority of the planet is oceanic, and these aliens have not yet developed the technology to extract—"

"Not yet."

"Well, it could take millions of years to get to that point."

"Millions of—ha!" Jerry brandishes a control orb, and as he fingers it another report scrolls into view. He mutters some of the highlights to himself. "Metallurgy, 700 years...mechanization, 28 years...okay, here it is: petroleum extraction: eleven years. Eleven years! In just eleven Xxzzrrrvan years they've gotten to the point where they're sucking over a trillion oobalings out of the ground."

Phthsspitty-snapp blinks. "But still, they probably...wow. How does that happen?"

"Come on, I know you had a class in technologification."

"I had trouble with that class. We had this professor, Dr. Zingpfft, who—"

"Yeah, yeah. But don't you remember? I bet you had a test question, 'identify four factors affecting the pace of technologification.'"

Phthsspitty-snapp shrugs.

"Rotation? Orbit? Especially rotation. This is a pretty small planet, and it's spinning pretty fast, so they cram ten days into every Xxzzrrrvan day. Their concept of time differs from ours."

Phthsspitty-snapp glares at him. "So? They haven't even moved past the continental shelves."

"Damn it, you haven't been paying attention, have you?" The probe lurches forward again, and he steers it southward, out over the sea, at the same time setting the display to highlight petroleum extraction rigs. They glow green, clustered thickly just off the coast, then petering out as the water gets deeper. But not petering out completely. "Water depth," Jerry says, and numbers pop up all over the sea. "What do you notice?" he asks.

She sighs. "All right. A few of them are in pretty deep water." She shakes her head and shoots him a glare. "Are you saying you'll recommend species extinction?"

"I'm saying we can recommend whatever we want, but the Board is going to do what it wants. They're going to do the same thing they always do in such cases." The same thing they did on Botruntun, he thinks grimly. A similar moment on that planet comes back to him, a moment after he had spent hours cruising its skies, measuring vast clouds of black smoke and scanning open canals of petroleum flowing from the deserts and oceans into the cities. Their red sun was setting when he found a massive continent's main canal, five iksiks across, the carcasses of lesser species scattered here and there along its shores. Dejected, he flew into the city and came across a parade of Botruntions weaving down a plastic street, all of them waving their seven tails and talking about the sun in that operatic language. He felt a stab of grief, but a surge of inspiration quickly followed. It was easy to mislead the

Exploratory Board into thinking Botruntun's other sentient species—squat, cave-dwelling marsupials of the polar regions— was to blame. Unfortunately, it was just as easy for the Board to uncover the ruse. During the tedious flurry of scandal that erupted, the atmosphere of Botruntun suddenly became poisonous to those operatic reptiles, and they quickly died out, leaving the planet to the arctic marsupials, who would be monitored eternally for any signs of developing a taste for petroleum. Not that there would be much left. And after many years of working his way back up the ladder, Jerry would be allowed to participate in another expedition, under close scrutiny. He wonders now whether the Exploratory Board knew he would find another oil-hungry sentient species here. What better test of his loyalty?

This time he feels a stab of anger. He curses the Exploratory Board, wishing their shoes to be infested with the thorn-wielding parasitic chinchillas of Dnzyland. He curses himself for ever wanting to get back into this profession when he could have just sold his story to the xxabloids and signed a book deal and let Xxollywood make whatever movie of his life it wanted to make. But instead of sitting with his feet up by a pool in the backyard of a palatial plastic house along the coast of the Xxacific, he is light years from home, strapped into a cramped probe that is starting to smell a little sweaty.

"What are you doing?" Phthsspitty-snapp asks, as the probe flutters down, gaining forward speed as it approaches the ground. Dark vegetation and glinting waterways slip past below them, and then they are over open water, still accelerating, dodging the tops of occasional oil rigs. Jerry taps the control orb and a little number pops up in the lower corner of the display. "What's that?" Phthsspitty-snapp asks.

Instead of answering, Jerry taps the orb again and the number gains a label: Ocean Depth. The number shifts and jumps, trending gradually upward, then begins rising steeply, at which point Jerry points the probe skyward until a vast swath of sea lies below them. A quick fiddle with the control orb and bright dots highlight the oil rigs. The probe dives again, closing on the southernmost dot, which quickly grows to become another spindly behemoth like the one they visited before. The depth sounder shows 22,345 vovaws, roughly equivalent to 4,132 feet. Jerry circles the rig once, then plunges the probe into the water. A tall metallic column, encrusted with aquatic invertebrates, hangs below the center of the rig, and Jerry spirals around it, following it into the depths. The waters darken, and he flicks on the illuminators.

At the bottom, he parks the probe at a distance that gives them a good view of the wellhead. "Impressive," he mutters.

Phthsspitty-snapp shakes her head. "Really?"

"What they've managed to do with crude technology," he says, pushing the probe forward and picking up the control orb. Red text begins flashing at the top of the display.

"Weapons systems? What are you...?"

"Just taking a closer look," Jerry says, and blasts the side of the metal column, leaving a neat hole just big enough for the probe to slip through. The interior is complicated, but with a little more blasting he finds a drill pipe full of thick black oil.

The preceding narrative serves to figuratively advance the hypothetical child's hypothetical toy black horse far ahead of the hypothetical toy white horse. As user of Oily, you understand that it is important not to forget the hypothetical toy brown horse of Gravy and Hmmm, even though it may be much smaller, and that it would be unjust for the child to neglect the white horse (understanding also that children often feel sorry for neglected toys). Advancing the horse of Gravy and Hmmm is a simple matter of shifting point of view to the bridge of the mother ship, where Hmmm has just declared, "I've seen enough" before striding to a supply cabinet near the exit. He grasps the handle and tries to twist it. He can see through a glass panel to several space suits hanging inside, but the damned door won't open. "How does this thing work?"

Gravy watches for a moment, seeming to enjoy Hmmm's confusion. "Why do you need one of those?"

"Just tell me how to open the bloody cabinet, lieutenant!" Hmmm says, and as user of Oily you understand that an alien is unlikely to have a British accent, but you also understand that a character such as Hmmm would have the alien equivalent of a British accent.

"You really only need those if there's a loss of cabin pressure," Gravy says. "Unless you're planning to leave the ship."

"I most certainly am. I'll be taking a probe down to the surface. Now tell me how to open the bloody cabinet!"

"The instructions are printed on the door."

"I don't have time to—'In case of emergency, break glass.' Well, I'd say this was an emergency!" Hmmm clenches his jaw and strikes the glass with his hand, then winces and does a little dance.

"There's a little hammer on a chain there," Gravy points out. "But—"

Before he can continue, Hmmm picks up the hammer and throws it into the glass, which obligingly shatters. "Now," he says, poking tentatively at the remaining shards.

"You don't need a suit to take a probe down." Sighing, Gravy stands up and stretches. "Come on," he says, "I'll show you."

"Yes, do. Put the ship on autopilot and lead the way," Hmmm says, blocking the exit and gazing at the console expectantly.

Gravy squeezes past him. "It's been on autopilot for several hours. Let's go."

As user of Oily, you accept and understand the need for patience; the creator of Oily accepts and understands his obligation to make your patience worthwhile. In other words, the creator of Oily understands the need to bring the imaginary toy horse in the imaginary child's imaginary race to a narrative finish line (although "finish line" is an inadequate symbol in this allegory, as it implies that the narrative will soon end; it may be necessary to think of the imaginary race as merely one heat in a series of races). ("Finish line," on the other hand, does imply a certain level of excitement, not dissimilar to the sort of excitement delivered by a narrative high point; "finish line" thus need not be discarded.) As user of Oily, you may wish to imagine the imaginary child's toy horses "running" neck and neck near the edge of an imaginary living room rug whose perimeter serves as the finish line. The white horse of characters Warren and Penny surges forward a bit as the narrative describes their hurried exit from the clinic, Penny saying, "What a jerk," as they walk to the car, Warren shaking his head with a sneer: "Ask your doctor about Sunshaya™."

"If I am depressed, it's because I'm sick," Penny says. "Not the other way around."

"Right."

They get settled in the car, and when Warren starts turning his head to back out, Penny puts a hand up by his cheek. "You believe me, right?" she asks. "You know this is not all in my head."

"Of course," he says, but as he begins the drive homeward he remembers how a pile of ungraded exams used to torture her, how she would nurse a cold or a sprained ankle as if it were life-threatening, how many classes she would cancel at the last minute. It occurred to him sometimes, in dark moments, that she had simply decided to retire from life. What proof does he have that her joints ache or that she is nauseated? "Of course," he says again.

The next day, Warren takes his usual morning expedition to the levee, and as always he keeps an eye out for night herons, egrets, terns, mullet and gar, sliders and snappers. But he walks a bit too briskly, not quite admitting to himself why he chose a white tee shirt and a red baseball cap. He sits on the slope of the levee in a spot he has visited many times, and as so often happens he falls into a reverie. This time, though, he has chosen the spot for a reason, and the reverie has nothing to do with urban ecology or the way a heron steps ashore before swallowing its fishy prey. Maybe they can read minds, he thinks. Maybe they scanned the whole planet and his thoughts were the most promising and so they dropped their spaceship down beside him in this very spot. Or if they can't read minds, maybe their medical technology detects pain and other bodily sensations, which might show up as green and red and blue zones on some sort of body scan. How could a civilization that has developed such advanced space travel not have such a device? And another device that takes a few samples and readings and such to determine within seconds what is wrong with a person? And another, or maybe the same one, that concocts and injects precisely formulated medications to effect a cure? He resists the temptation of imagining Penny throwing the covers aside and striding springily outside to spread her arms and spin around, smiling at the sky, because he is realistic enough to figure even alien cures might take a few days to work. Here I am, he thinks loudly. Right where you found me yesterday. I'm pretty conspicuous here on the green grass. Come on down. A belted kingfisher flies past, chattering reproachfully.

He hears the groaning the moment he gets through the front door. Running to the bedroom, he knows he is the worst person for ever thinking an alien brain scan might find that she has been faking this illness. Not Penny. Someone else maybe, but not Penny. "It's really bad today," she sobs as he rushes to put his arm around her where she sits on the edge of the bed, head down and vomit bowl between her feet. "Look at my arms." She holds them out, and he runs his fingers lightly over the patches of rash covering the tender underside of her forearms.

"It's on your neck and cheek, too," he tells her. "Does it itch this time?"

"Not really." She gives him a fearful look then tries to smile. "Think Sunshaya™ would take care of this?"

He fetches Phenergan®, a cool cloth, and ginger tea, then spreads organic lotion over the rash. She asks for music and he pulls up his play list of Corelli™ and Telemann™. She lies back on a bank of pillows, moaning and fretting until the Phenergan® makes her start to doze.

Warren will spend the day at work alone, grading papers, and lonely at home afterwards, sweeping the floor, cleaning the bathroom, and eating dinner by himself. He'll have plenty of time to lambaste himself for being oafish, almost concluding that his cruel doubts brought on Penny's flare-up.

When she wakes up he'll make her the best cup of ginger tea he has ever made, and he'll study her face as she sips from it. *I would do the same for you*, she seems to be thinking. *It's what we signed up for.* He'll show her half a smile, thinking, *I know you would. Some day you might have to.* He'll wonder if he should fetch some saltines. "I think I could eat some crackers," she'll croak, and he'll say, "Thank God," springing into action.

Later they'll sit together in bed, pecking at laptops. When she emits a mournful "Oh no!" he'll lunge for the barf bowl. "No, it's not that," she'll say. "It says here that a rig exploded out in the Gulf. Some workers are missing, and the thing is still on fire."

As user of Oily, when you reach this point in the narrative, you will understand that your patience has been rewarded and the white horse corresponding to Warren and Penny wins by a nose.

C. Imagination: As user of Oily, you have the ability to read (see Article III.A), and you accept the role of imagination in reading a fanciful narrative such as Oily. It is not unreasonable to declare that all reading requires imagination, as it involves the translation of angular/curvilinear marks upon a contrasting surface into letters forming words forming sentences delivering information and/or ideas and/or expressions of emotion. Thus the following black glyphs upon this white page and/or screen gain significance: *"Oops," Jerry says, guiding the probe in a high holding pattern over the roaring flames and billowing smoke.* The process by which the glyphs gain significance occurs nearly instantaneously and consists of multiple operations, one or more of which requires imaginative thought.

Furthermore, as user of Oily you accept the role of your imagination in reading narrative texts in particular. In addition to imaginative translation of shapes on paper/screen into words, activation of those regions of the brain involved in visualization, auralization, olfactorization, tactilization, etc. is required of users of narrative. You accept your obligation to picture (for example) Phthsspitty-snapp rubbing her back arm where it thwacked the side of Jerry's seat during the wild, tumbling ride through the drill pipe from deep under the seabed to their weapon-assisted emergence at the top of the rig, and to hear her say "Did you mean to do that?" and further hear the remainder of an exchange between Phthsspitty-snapp and Jerry, beginning with Jerry's reply of "Yes and no. I meant to rupture the drill pipe. I didn't mean to cause an explosion" and continuing with Phthsspitty-snapp's "I think you probably killed a few of them" (while visualizing her "zooming in the video on a few aliens bobbing in the water near the rig, waving at a boat approaching from the north").

Jerry sighs. "Well, I didn't mean to. The whole structure is so fragile!"

"What were you thinking?" Phthsspitty-snapp asks. "I thought you were on their side."

"I am! You don't get it? It's a long shot, but it could save them."

"You've had a long day. Maybe you should head back to the mother ship," Phthsspitty-snapp says.

"Very funny. No, look—you've got to learn to think like the Exploratory Board."

"Well, I can see that the Board is going to want to exterminate this species."

"Unless...?"

"Unless...we can convince them not to?"

"By...?"

"By convincing them that their petroleum extraction is limited?"

"Limited because...? Come on, you were the one who suggested it before."

"Limited because...they don't have the technology to extract petroleum out past the continental shelves."

"Do you get it now?" Jerry asks, gesturing toward the video display, where the flaming rig is beginning to list steeply. "The ones we killed—I killed, without meaning to—their deaths are not in vain. If my plan—our plan—works, they'll be heroes."

You accept that in order for your use of Oily to be successful you must activate your imagination and that the text of Oily functions as a series of instructions to your imagination, directing you for example to visualize Phthsspitty-snapp studying the flaming rig as the probe rises slowly into the night sky, the conflagration casting a flickering light over the surrounding sea. It begins to look like a single candle in a vast darkness as the probe reaches greater heights. Jerry ignores Phthsspitty-snapp and the image of the disaster, busying himself with the navigation orb. Phthsspitty-snapp blinks when the monitor goes green, showing the planetary map the probe has been piecing together over the course of the expedition. Jerry studies the map, scrolling to the north and east, zooming in and out, turning overlays on and off. It looks like he is targeting an area off the arctic coast of the continent far to the east and north, where earlier they saw another vast cluster of rigs. "What are you doing?" she asks.

"Choosing our next destination."

Phthsspitty-snapp rolls her eyes. "I realize that," she says. "I guess I should have asked, 'where are we going?'"

"Right...here." Jerry gives the navigation orb one last poke, drawing a bead on one of the outermost rigs of the northern sea. "And we'll go half-speed, maybe even quarter-speed. That'll give us some time to work on the report, take a nap or two, stretch our legs."

"Why?"

"Well, the preliminary report is due in about seventeen hours, and I'm feeling a bit tired."

"You knew what I meant. Why are we going there?"

Narratives such as the text of Oily are often evaluated on the basis of the quality and clarity of their instruction to users' imaginations, particularly when the narrative is classified as science fiction. As user of Oily, however, you accept your obligation to make earnest efforts to use your imagination to fill gaps in the narrative. All narrative texts are loosely woven, imperfect efforts to describe events, circumstances, characters, objects, actions, thoughts, emotions, and other features of experience; they are approximations. As user of Oily, you accept your obligation to complete the narrative yourself. Extending the "loosely woven" analogy, you accept your obligation to be shown a net and imagine a blanket. Introducing a different analogy, you accept your obligation to be shown a sketch and imagine a painting. "Filling gaps" in a narrative requires not just imagination, but also a certain amount of knowledge. The creator of Oily assumes that users of Oily possess knowledge of, for example, the demise of the Deepwater Horizon petroleum extraction rig in the Gulf of Mexico in 2010, which informs users' use of Oily. Furthermore, knowledge of the Deepwater Horizon disaster (and/or similar disasters) facilitates the visualization of Oily's similar (but entirely fictional) Gulf-of-Mexico-oil-rig disaster, whose similarity to British Petroleum's Deepwater Horizon disaster could conceivably be entirely coincidental, especially considering the fact that there has been no indication that aliens of any size or type contributed in any way to that disaster. In fact, such a scenario is manifestly improbable, as is the likelihood that the creator of Oily was privy to a conversation between aliens as they left the scene of the conflagration, a conversation that resumes with Jerry the Exploratory-Board employee saying, "All right," whereupon he stops smiling and says, "Did you have a good history class?"

"I had two," Phthsspitty-snapp says. "Galactic History and History of Exploration."

"Okay. So what happened when we first started drilling for petroleum on a moon? A Xxzzrrrvan moon. The first off-planet extraction."

"On Circulon or Crescenta?"

"The one we did first, whichever one that was."

"Circulon. Well, at the time Xxzzrrrva had yet to develop seismic laser technology, and Viceroy Yo-Yo was lead engineer. He was criticized for bringing more men and equipment than—"

"Yeah, yeah," Jerry says. "Fast forward. Look at the big picture."

"Big picture. All right. Well...eventually three networks of intersecting extractors pulled something like a trillion oobalings from Circulon, which I think took—"

"Headlines!" Jerry says. "What happened that made headlines?"

The console emits a shrill tone, making Phthsspitty-snapp jump. A red message flashes on the monitor. "Evasive maneuver?" Jerry says. "That's ridiculous. False alarm." He overrides the autopilot and cancels the maneuver. No sooner has he done so than a massive stapling sound shakes the probe and it begins a steep, erratic descent. "Battle stations!" Jerry shouts.

"Battle stations!?"

Jerry takes a control orb in each hand and leans toward the monitor, which flashes through a dizzying series of screens and views as he works feverishly.

"Where's my battle station?" Phthsspitty-snapp yells. "What do I do?"

"Hold on!" The lights go off, except for a little blue standby indicator, and the probe drops straight down, nose first. After a few moments Phthsspitty-snapp hears a faint splash, and the probe's descent slows abruptly.

"What the hell is happening?" she whispers.

"We're hiding," Jerry whispers. He holds up one hand. "It's pretty shallow here, so we should be...." The probe bumps down softly, then rolls over a few times, finally coming to rest at an uncomfortable half-sideways angle.

"Who are we hiding from?"

"Whoever shot us down."

"Shot us down. Shot us down? Do the aliens have a military? Oh God, there's like a whole swarm of giants with mechanical weapons coming after us, isn't there? Why did you have to attack their petroleum extraction site like that?"

VI. USER CONDUCT

A. Vocal Performance: As user of Oily, you are not permitted to enact, perform, or read aloud any portion of Oily. The intent of this clause, however, is not to prohibit permissible exceptions. Users who happen to have audible reactions to the text of Oily while reading silently may recite brief portions of the text in order to explain their guffaws, gasps, tongue clucks, and/or exclamations. Should users, for example, say "Ha!" while eating celery or gourmet popcorn in bed beside their significant other(s), it is permissible to respond to the aforementioned other(s)'s queries by saying, "I just found out who shot down the probe. There's this stuffy bureaucrat named Hmmm, and he's been following the other aliens after they blew up an oil rig...well here, it goes like this: '"What the hell are you doing?" Gravy shouts, raising a hand to knock Hmmm aside, then thinking better of it.' Gravy's the pilot of the mother ship. Anyway, then it goes, '"I am merely protecting the interests of our Exploratory Board and ultimately our planet," Hmmm says calmly.

"By killing two members of our crew?"

"Can you confirm their deaths?" Hmmm asks, studying the video display. "How may we locate the wreckage?"

"Confirm their deaths? Holy excrement. That's not what we need to do." Gravy snatches up a control orb and taps it rapidly. The words "RESCUE MODE" flash in white at the top of the screen. He studies a replay of the energy burst Hmmm fired striking the back of Jerry's probe and its dark shadow tumbling erratically into blackness.

"Can you pinpoint their location?" Hmmm asks, idling picking up his co-pilot control orb.

"It's given me a five-hundred square iksik area with various zones of probability," Gravy sighs.

"This is not responding," Hmmm says, tapping the orb hard.

Gravy waves one hand casually. "I've disconnected co-pilot controls," he says. "No more surprises."

"I merely wish to make some calculations."

"Use your mini-device."

Hmmm frowns and pulls a smaller orb from his breast pocket. As the probe dives toward the surface of the planet—probably more steeply than necessary—and begins flying a search pattern, he pecks at the orb. "Five million oobalings per hour," he says indignantly. "Five million oobalings per hour, just pouring out into the sea.'"

Under normal circumstances, vocal recitations from the text of Oily should not exceed the approximate length of the above example, although it is permissible to recite the entire text of Oily in private to oneself and/or one other person, who may for example be a spouse, child, or elderly relative. The creator of Oily understands the therapeutic value of reading aloud, having been read aloud to as a child by his parents and as an adult by his spouse, whose name is not Penny and who is not ill like Penny but who also benefits from being read to by the creator of Oily, not from Oily itself but from other books, whose titles he won't mention just in case their creators are litigious and/or ill-tempered.

Users who recite the entire text of Oily (or lengthy portions thereof) to ill or elderly patients not related by blood or marriage and receive compensation for their recitation of the text are, strictly speaking, required to comply with regulations regarding payment of royalties for public performances of copyrighted works of art. Not that the creator of Oily expects that to be a problem. But you can't be too careful.

These stipulations and all other stipulations made by this TOU pertain equally to the free (gratis) electronic version of Oily and the reasonably priced print-on-demand version, as well as to all future gratis and retail versions, and the creator of Oily wants users to know that he is not motivated by a desire for monetary compensation, which should be obvious considering his decision to make Oily available for free online.

By clicking "Agree" below, users accept their responsibility to ensure that any vocal performance of the text of Oily is private. Exceptions for educational purposes are permissible, although the right of users to use Oily for educational purposes is not unlimited. Educators may recite the text of Oily in educational settings, provided they ensure that no student or other person creates a recording of the text for non-educational purposes. Educators may require students to recite from Oily, for example calling upon a young man to read a portion starting on page 93, which begins, "Phthsspitty-snapp can just make out Jerry's face nearby, faintly lit by the blue glow of the standby indicator. He seems to be listening intently, and so she follows suit. Without the usual hum and faint clickings of the probe's propulsion system and instruments, the silence seems loud. 'What the hell happened?' she whispers.

"'Something struck the rear portion of the probe,' he whispers back. 'Some kind of weapon, I think.'

'Who would do that?'

'Not sure.'

'Can we run an analysis?' She reaches for the console, but he puts out a hand to stop her.

'We need to avoid detection,' he says. 'Standby only until further notice.'

'Where are we?'

'We're half an iksik underwater, in a coastal region south of the city where we made landfall.'

'How long do we have to stay here?'

'The longer we wait, the better the chance we'll escape. You might as well get some sleep.'"

At this point an educator has no obligation to say, "All right. Thank you, Hunter," but it is suggested that an educator call upon various students, perhaps at this point saying, "Allison, would you continue?" Allison may clear her throat, sit up a little straighter, and recite the following: "Jerry closes his eyes, and as Phthsspitty-snapp watches, his face goes slack and his breathing slows. She can't help asking, 'Are you really asleep already?' He frowns, blinking, and gives her a glare. 'In our line of work it helps to be able to sleep on cue. Now leave me alone.' And again he dozes off within moments. Phthsspitty-snapp closes her eyes and tries to relax, but with the probe resting at an odd angle and all of the day's events swirling through her head, she only grows more alert. She starts to imagine the space-mail she will compose and send back to her mother on Xxzzrrrva if she ever gets a chance. It will be a long space-mail, beginning of course with some obligatory chattiness and inquiries after Mama's health and the winter weather, and then a gossipy paragraph about her grouchy partner and his checkered history, mitigated by assurances that he is perfectly nice and the rumors aren't true. No mention of his latest rebellion against the Exploratory Board. Then the paragraph that will make Mama put one hand to her face, eyes wide: 'I met an alien today. This planet is populated by billions of sentient aliens, basically Xxzzrrrvanoid but probably an iksik high. They have relatively advanced mechanics and electronics. Today I saw so much—huge ceramic roads full of giant vehicles, a metallic ship the size of a Xxzzrrrvan city, enormous primitive oil-extraction rigs. Yes, these aliens extract petroleum and use it as fuel and to make plastics and such, and they do so at a pretty high rate— billions of oobalings per day. I can't say too much, but as you can imagine, the Exploratory Board won't be too happy about this. I'm afraid species elimination will be the solution, which is a shame because...because....' Here Phthsspitty-snapp stops to think. Why is it such a shame? She has never liked to hear of species extinction but generally accepts it as a necessary evil, comforting herself with the usual Xxzzrrrvan rationale: the species in question is just one of many on the planet in question, their extraction and use of petroleum has damaged their planet, and (most of all) Xxzzrrrva's survival depends on using the petroleum, which would not have been there at all if not for ancient Xxzzrrrvans' planetary life-seeding projects. In fact, the species in question would not exist at all if not for the actions of long-ago Xxzzrrrvans. Such a rationale usually suffices, but today it rings hollow, maybe because she has met this species, has visited it in one of its houses. But that isn't it—she knows she wouldn't feel such passion if the aliens were cactus dogs or cannibalistic microbes."

Dramatization of the text of Oily is strictly limited to unrehearsed reenactments for educational purposes. Memorization of lines, elaborate blocking, and the use of prepared props and scenery are prohibited. In most instances, dramatizations taking place in auditoriums, gymnasiums, and cafeterias are subject to regulations regarding payment of royalties for public performances of copyrighted works of art, which require written permission and payment of fees. Audiences for reenactments must be no larger than the size of a typical grade-school or college class, and reenactments should typically take place in classrooms. Educators and others are responsible for ensuring that no unauthorized attendees witness the performance by (for example) looking through an uncovered window or open doorway. Despite these restrictions, educators are encouraged to assign roles to specific students, who are permitted to stand up and act out actions of characters as described in the text of Oily. An educator may, for example, ask a student named Shannon to "be" Phthsspitty-snapp and another student named Darryl to "be" Jerry in the following scene:

Phthsspitty-snapp notices the resumption of the probe's usual ambient sounds in her sleep, but doesn't fully awaken until the probe itself begins to move. Jerry leans forward, intent and grim as he pilots the probe slowly through sun-struck tea-colored water, dodging aquatic vegetation. "Where to?" she asks.

"We've got to find a place to hide."

"From whoever attacked us?"

"That's right."

"Any idea who it was?"

Jerry replies by tapping a control orb twice, causing text to scroll up on the monitor: *Damage Report/loss of material and fuel from rear fuselage/40% compromise of propulsion system. Cause: Weaponry. Type: Xxzzrrrvan energy pulse.*

Phthsspitty-snapp gasps. "Our own people?"

"Person. Have you met Councilor Hmmm?"

"What, that tall serious guy with the fancy gray hair? I've seen him, never spoken to him."

"I suspect he's the one who pulled the trigger."

"But why?"

"He's always been quick to assume I was up to no good," Jerry says. "Well, maybe not always. But ever since Botruntun. So he probably figured I was sabotaging Grawgraw's oil supply."

"You'd think he would call first."

"Like I said, quick to assume."

Phthsspitty-snapp stares at the video display, catching glimpses of sleek aquatic animals with silvery sides who flee at their approach. "And now he's looking for us?"

"Most likely. Unless he assumed he destroyed us. He's more likely to assume he didn't."

Phthsspitty-snapp shudders, wondering if Councilor Hmmm is just now drawing a bead on them.

"That water makes us a little harder to detect," Jerry says. "And it helps to go slowly and stay low. But what we really need is metal."

"To hide under?"

"Right."

They both stew for a while, watching the sunny bayou water for glimpses of wildlife—roundish animals with domelike shells, a wide variety of quick fish, and once in a while huge reptilians with short legs and long, toothy snouts hanging motionless near the surface, ignoring the passage of the black acorn. Fast boats move in both directions occasionally, and some sit still near the bank. Phthsspitty-snapp wonders what they are doing until she catches sight of a crude plastic rendition of a little fish following a nearly invisible string.

Individual educators may determine how long such dramatizations may continue. It is understood that sometimes educators have busy weekends and make insufficient plans for Monday's classes, and that with current trends toward block scheduling in American secondary education there may be considerable time to fill. Educators teaching classes filled with inquisitive, talkative students may halt the dramatization at this point and simply allow their classes to discuss the text of Oily. Educators who enjoy the sounds of their own voices may halt the dramatization at this point and simply launch a lengthy monologue which begins by pointing out obvious plot developments and features of the dramatized excerpt and continues with a lengthy digression about fishing and hunting. All educators should bear in mind that it is permissible to continue the dramatization, at this point asking that girl Linda who missed so much class last month to play the role of Hmmm and that badass Lance to play the role of Gravy:

High overhead, Hmmm and Gravy sit side-by-side at the console of their probe. "You will find that probe," Hmmm says, narrowing his eyes.

Gravy pilots the craft in and out of a thin layer of clouds, describing a lazy eight-mile loop. "We've been looking for it for a long time now. Like I said, you probably destroyed it."

"Then find the wreckage!"

"We'll return to the mother ship and I'll get the scanners going. It will take a while, though."

"That's not good enough. If that probe survived, we need to be in position to pursue it the moment it's detected. I know you can have your officers set up the scanning. Do you miss your ship, is that it? I understand a pilot's affection for his vessel, but you've also got to have devotion to your mission, and our mission is compromised by the actions of the occupants of that probe."

Gravy frowns petulantly. "They had names, you know. One of them was a young intern on her first voyage."

"And the other one put her in danger by an act of sabotage and treason," Hmmm replies, jabbing the air with one finger.

"We'll make one more sweep," Gravy says, and forces the probe into an uncomfortably steep dive back toward the coastal area below.

Hmmm clenches his jaw and closes his eyes, but opens them at the sound of an insistent beeping from the console. "What's that?" he asks, staring at a small glowing rectangle in front of Gravy.

Gravy eases out of the steep dive and holds the probe steady several iksiks above a narrow waterway. "It's a pretty faint reading," he says. "But it looks like Xxzzrrrvan propulsion."

"I don't feel safe," Phthsspitty-snapp tells Jerry. "Are you scanning for metal?"

"There's not much infrastructure out here," Jerry says. "But I think we'll be coming to some roadways soon." He flicks on the sensors, which at first show only small flecks of metal trash here and there on the bottom of the bayou, but then they come upon two boats fishing near the bank. "One of them is metallic," Jerry says, surprised. "I thought they would be organic cellulose like the one we saw earlier." He slows, turning the probe and parking it under the metallic boat.

"What's the other one made of?" Phthsspitty-snapp asks.

"Some sort of petroleum-derived thermoplastic."

They watch a purplish fishing lure swim up to the boat, wriggling provocatively. It leaves the water, then reappears with a plop fifty yards away.

"Pinpoint the location!" Hmmm cries.

"Signal's gone," Gravy says, working the control orb.

"Nevertheless, I'm sure our instruments can pinpoint the last location of the signal, perhaps calculate its velocity and heading, and guide us to the proper coordinates. What are you doing? Where are you going? Explain yourself, captain!"

Gravy eases the probe to a halt between the tops of trees lining a murky, narrow waterway. "It was right about here. Probably traveling underwater in an effort to avoid detection. Moving northward rather slowly."

"We've got to keep moving," Jerry says, after he and Phthsspitty-snapp have watched the purple lure swim back dozens of times.

"But this is safe, right?" Phthsspitty-snapp says. "And this guy will probably start moving soon."

"I'm starting to doubt that," Jerry says, nudging the probe around to face the way they had come. "And who knows which way he'll go?"

"But at least we're safe," she points out, doing her best not to sound worried.

"Here comes one," Jerry says, focusing video on a commotion to the south. A boat similar to the one they are parked under comes bounding along, casting spray to each side. "Thermoplastic," Jerry says dismissively, and they watch the underside of the boat zip past, leaving a turbulence that makes the probe and the vessel above it rock and bob in unison.

Before heading northward, Gravy spends a moment studying the alien seated on the metallic vessel parked by the shore. It is gigantic, clothed in loose geometric patches of fabric, and it looks just like a Xxzzrrrvan turned sideways. It manipulates a stiff whip threaded with translucent string and fitted with a mechanical winch. Gravy loves the clean emptiness and darkness of space, loves big spaceships and interstellar navigation, and as a pilot he has a certain obligation to call planets dirtballs and rocks and to roll his eyes whenever scientists launch into intricate rhapsodies on their topographies, floras, and faunas. But he finds himself wishing he could take a probe down to every planet and get this close to every alien species.

As luck would have it, a metallic boat comes along just as Gravy pauses to study the alien, and Jerry executes a smooth maneuver, pushing the probe out into the waterway as the boat passes, accelerating to match its velocity. An alert pops up on Gravy's monitor. "What's that?" Hmmm yells. "It's the signal!"

Gravy curses, jabbing at a control orb. "It's gone. No signal."

Hmmm leans toward the console. "Show me the trajectory of the signal," he says, and Gravy complies. "Now superimpose the trajectory on synchronous video."

"Oops," Gravy says, dropping the control orb. "Just a second."

"Hurry up, captain!" Hmmm says.

"Got it. Let's see here...."

Hmmm pushes his face even closer to the display. "There. You see? They're following that alien vessel, hiding beneath it."

"You're right, Councilor."

Hmmm turns his reddening face to Gravy, veins popping. "Well, get going!"

The water beneath the alien vessel is turbulent and noisy. Jerry leans forward, working intently to keep the probe centered under the speeding object. "How far do you suppose this'll take us?" Phthsspitty-snapp says loudly.

Jerry just shakes his head and takes his hand off the accelerator just long enough to wave toward the console. "Give me the ceramics overlay."

She taps her control orb a few times, though nothing changes on the monitor. "No ceramics," she says.

"Not yet."

"What are you looking for?"

"Think about it."

Educators whose students clamor for chances to have turns playing roles in Oily's narrative accept their obligation to feel fortunate to have such students, and to allow such students to crouch under desks and/or other furniture with their texts while playing the roles of Phthsspitty-snapp and Jerry and/or perch atop desks and/or other furniture while playing the roles of Gravy and Hmmm. Such educators furthermore accept their obligation to resist such students' requests for more formal performances, involving, for example, elaborate plywood mockups of Xxzzrrrvan probes, keeping in mind the restrictions articulated above. The use of costumes for any non-educational purpose is prohibited, even in the unlikely and/or likely event that Oily becomes a bestselling product that is adapted for film and/or television, resulting in mass production of Oily Halloween costumes for children and/or adolescents and/or adults. Potential publishers should note that the creator of Oily fully understands and adheres to all federal and local regulations regarding such matters, for "It's a minefield out there, and writers who don't know all of the ins and outs are liabilities," according to at least one literary agent. By clicking AGREE below, all users, including potential publishers, acknowledge that the creator of Oily knows all of the ins and outs.

B. Trademarks and Copyright: As user of Oily, you accept your obligation to avoid all violations of trademark and copyright. Such violations include but are not limited to composition of narratives (including but not limited to narrative films, plays, short stories, poems, novels, comic books, textbooks, travel guides, letters, emails, web sites, photo essays, ballets, symphonies, paintings, statuary, memoirs, telephone directories, advertisements, songs, cookbooks, diaries, and self-help manuals) based in whole or substantial part upon the narrative of Oily; depictions of characters, objects, scenes, and/or circumstances unique to Oily; use of any part of the text of Oily in promotional materials for any literary and/or nonliterary product, event, and/or person; and use and/or depiction and/or display of any part of Oily, including its front or back cover and/or jacket and any inside page, including the blank pages at the end.

In addition, major and/or minor characters featured in Oily are covered by trademark and copyright, and users must under no circumstances create narrative works or performances featuring characters based upon characters featured in Oily. The creator of Oily accepts the possibility of coincidence, within limits. For example, a user of Oily who writes a short story featuring a scientist named Jerry is unlikely to face a lawsuit, provided there is sufficient contrast between the character traits, dialogue/monologue, and/or experiences of Oily's Jerry the alien scientist (Jerry™) and the user's Jerry the alien and/or non-alien scientist (Jerry). If Jerry, like Jerry™, has a history of humane, maverick behavior (e.g., misdirecting a powerful bureaucratic government agency in order to save an alien species), users may be in violation of trademark regulations.

Furthermore, character names unique to Oily are protected by trademark. Although names such as Jerry, Warren, and Penny may be used by users and/or non-users of Oily (some of whom may themselves be named Jerry, Warren, or Penny) without restrictions beyond those described above, accidental and/or intentional use of names such as Hmmm™ and Gravy™ in any public context violates trademark (which is not to say that users and/or non-users may not use the words hmmm and gravy in public context; e.g., the words "Hmmm, let's see...I think I will pour a certain amount of gravy upon these mashed potatoes," even if used in public, for-profit documents, do not violate trademark or copyright).

As user of Oily, you understand that character names will not bear the trademark notation (™) when appearing in the text of Oily. The creator of Oily ascertains that the notation would distract from the narrative, a point he demonstrates by providing the following specially altered excerpt:

Gravy™ sets off after the alien vessel, following its track along the water around a slight bend in the bayou, and soon enough it comes into view. Two aliens in hats occupy the vessel, one of them sitting at a small control console. "Get closer," Hmmm™ commands, and Gravy™ takes the probe down, matching its speed to the speed of the boat. "Closer!" Hmmm™ shouts.

"I can't risk detection," Gravy™ says. "The protocols dictate that even in—"

Hmmm™ points toward the water. "Down there!"

"Sir, if we just wait a short while, the alien vessel is sure to stop, or the waterway will narrow to the point where they must slow down. It's already narrowing somewhat."

Hmmm™ turns to Gravy™, bearing a sarcastic grimace on his reddened face. "It's about time you called me 'sir,'" he says. "Now do it again and take us under water!"

"I've thought about it," Phthsspitty-snapp™ says at around the same time. "You're looking for a roadway?"

"Right," Jerry™ says.

"But won't we be exposed?"

Jerry™ smiles. "You haven't thought it through all the way. Didn't they teach you how to improvise?"

"Well, there was an emphasis on critical thinking...?"

A rectangular blob appears on the monitor, growing quickly as the probe speeds upstream. "That's good," Jerry™

says, leaning toward the monitor, hands ready. "What about quick thinking?"

Gravy™ keeps the probe in the turbulent fluid behind the alien boat longer than he has to, struggling with the controls as if he were just out of flight school. At last he speeds up and breaks into smoother water under the boat. "There they are!" Hmmm™ cries, and puts his finger up to the wavering black shape in the corner of the monitor.

"Where?" Gravy™ says sarcastically.

Hmmm™ pecks at the console, and a message pops up on the monitor: *Are you sure you want to arm weapons systems? Okay/Cancel.*

Gravy™ does his own pecking. *Cancel.* "I can't let you do that, sir," he says.

"I'm in charge here," Hmmm™ says.

"No, you are not. As captain of the mother ship and all supplementary vessels, including this probe, I have authority over all personnel aboard the mother ship and all supplementary vessels."

"I see," Hmmm™ says, a mean twinkle lighting up one eye. "And can *you* get *me* fired?"

Gravy™ sighs, shaking his head, and holds up both hands in the universal signal for surrender, combining it with the nearly-identical universal signal for "fine, but you won't get any help from me." Hmmm™ resumes tapping at the console with a hint of glee.

"Hold on tight," Jerry™ says as the rectangular blob crossing the waterway fills the screen.

Phthsspitty-snapp™ just opens her eyes wide and points at the red text flashing at the top of the monitor: *Evasive Maneuver.* She makes an incoherent sound. Jerry™ slaps at the console, canceling the maneuver, and leans into a sharp turn to the right. Phthsspitty-snapp™'s eyes are mostly closed for the next few seconds, but as the probe bursts into the air she catches glimpses of sunlight and some sort of structure covered by the pink glow and black lines of metallic and ceramic overlays. Then the probe accelerates and settles into a new straight path. She hears a lot of loud humming and buzzing, and opening her eyes reveals a thin bar of sunlight ahead, a broad black surface speeding past below, and a complex pink structure hovering overhead. "Turn off the overlays," Jerry™ says. Phthsspitty-snapp™ taps a control orb and the pink and black highlights fall away.

"Ceramic roadway," Phthsspitty-snapp™ says slowly, piecing it together. "Are we under a vehicle?"

"You got it," Jerry™ says.

At about the same time, Hmmm™ is screaming at Gravy™— "After them!"—like some sort of B-movie villain. Gravy™ carefully steers the probe toward the bank, executing a U-turn at the same time, and begins dodging through dark decaying limbs and stumps in the shallows, making his way toward the bridge. "Faster!" Hmmm™ cries, all dastardly.

"Avoid detection at all costs," Gravy™ reminds him.

Hmmm™ takes umbrage and begins speechifying. "That is not a direct quote from mission protocol," he huffs. "And like so many individual policies within the protocol, it is superseded by statements in Article 17.3.1 regarding the preservation of mission integrity. Remember the famous example? 'Unless the ship is on fire.' Like most famous examples, it is reductive, but nevertheless—"

"There they are," Gravy™ says, now guiding the probe at high speed just above a broad ceramic roadway. Vehicles whip past in the other direction, buffeting the probe.

"Allow me," Hmmm™ says, tapping at a control orb until crosshairs glow in the middle of the video display. "Hold her steady, captain."

"I'll get closer," Gravy™ says helpfully, causing the probe to surge toward the vehicle ahead and the dark spot flying beneath it. The crosshairs dance and bobble around Hmmm™'s target.

That pesky *Evasive Maneuver* message flashes on the screen of Jerry™'s probe. Jerry™ swears, Phthsspitty-snapp™ cringes, and the probe veers out from under the vehicle, spiraling up into the sky at an acute angle. Timothy™, the driver of the 2007 Ford Focus under which Jerry™ and Phthsspitty-snapp™ have been hiding, feels the steering wheel jerk a bit and hears a loud hum from his right front tire. Within seconds the hum turns into a chainsaw buzz, then a violent thumping. He pulls over, gets out, and trots around the Focus to study the shredded tire. "It looks like someone burned a hole in it," a tire guy will tell Timothy™ a couple of hours later, and they will both shake their heads slowly.

production of novels of other genres and in the production of films, paintings, ballets, telephone directories, etc. Despite significant differences from the tone, intent, content, theme, and details of Oily, the following text, for example, would qualify as plagiarism if it were to appear in a user's artifact and/or performance:

Larry clenches his teeth, causing a handsome muscle to bulge at the base of his jaw, and fights to rein in the wildly bucking probe as it streaks skyward. "Oh, Larry!" Snappity-fizz cries, feeling as if the violent forces of acceleration have pressed the words from her throat.

"I'll protect you," Larry says huskily, cracking half a smile even as he pushes the probe into a steep dive toward the roadway far below.

"Perhaps we should simply surrender," Snappity-fizz murmurs, immediately covering her sensuous lips as if to smother the words she has already uttered.

"Surrender?" Larry scoffs, all macho and such. He just shakes his head, for there is no time to talk. Rapidly filling the monitor is the monstrous form of a huge alien vehicle, a gigantic rectangular trailer towed by a gleaming orange machine with many wheels. Snappity-fizz gasps, afraid Larry will drive the probe through the metallic shell of the vehicle, but at the last moment he brings the probe up short and parks it neatly on a greasy metal beam between truck and trailer.

"Oh, that was masterful," Snappity-fizz gushes, unable to keep her eyes off of Larry's muscular forearms. The image of his strength makes her feel weak, ironically. "But are we safe?"

"Probably not," Larry says coolly.

Meanwhile, the dastardly Uh-huh and his reluctant aide Saucy speed along in their own probe high above the roadway. "Where are they?" Uh-huh demands. "Use some fancy technological devices whose complexity would baffle humans to track them down."

"That's what I'm doing," Saucy mutters, working the console. "But a few moments, filled with mystifying beeps and flashes, will pass before I can pinpoint their location."

"Is there no signal emitted by their propulsion system?" Uh-huh cries. "If so, you must again calculate the trajectory of the most recent signal and triangulate their location thusly."

Without answering, Saucy executes a dive nearly as precipitous as that performed moments ago by Larry. He snaps it off and holds the probe in a hover over the road, just above the tops of the tallest vehicles that speed past below them. "Trajectory ends here," he says.

"So again the fiends fly low beneath one of these primitive vehicles," Uh-huh muses, eyes narrowed to evil slits. "After them!"

"Oh, Larry," Snappity-fizz sighs, admiring her courageous mentor's manly profile. "Shall we ever see the beautiful shores of Lake Kkkkrrakakak again?" She closes her winsome eyes and visits those gently curving shores in her mind, sharing a picnic of Xxzzrrrvan prunes, Plahplahplah seeds, and yellow-flower wine with the tautly muscled man by her side.

"Brace yourself," Larry barks. The bumping and jostling of the probe as it rests on the back of the truck intensifies, and the probe rolls a quarter-turn to the left, leaving them at an uncomfortable angle for a moment. Snappity-fizz blinks up at Larry, who reaches down a hand to steady himself against her seat. She studies his strong hand for a moment, struggling to gather the courage to place her own delicate hand with his there, but before she can do so the probe rolls a little further and tumbles off of the truck, landing roughly on the gritty surface below.

"Oh dear!" Snappity-fizz gasps, but Larry merely leans toward the console, studying an electronic diagram. His manly calm makes her regret her girlish gasp.

"Any sign of them?" Uh-huh asks, for the third time, and Saucy shakes his head. "How are we to know whether they have taken one of these other pathways?" Uh-huh says, noting a curving roadway that veers off to the right. At about the same time, Saucy and Uh-huh's probe speed past Larry and Snappity-fizz's probe lying in the middle of the road, looking to the casual observer like a stray bit of plastic or rubber litter and to aliens streaking past at twice the speed of traffic like one flat blob of tar among many (not that either alien streaking past at twice the speed of traffic notices).

"Damn," Larry says, in a very manly fashion.

"What is it?" Snappity-fizz asks, eyes wide and very feminine.

"Whoever's chasing us just passed right over our heads."

"Oh Larry, I'm scared!" Snappity-fizz cries.

"It's all right, darlin'," he says, sounding a bit like John Wayne or Elvis Presley. "At least we know where they are. They're so close to the ground that when we make a move they probably won't detect it, or if they do it'll take them a while to get back here, and by then we'll be gone."

"This is sheer folly," Uh-huh declares. "I don't believe we'll find them in this fashion."

Saucy just shrugs and keeps going. "I suggest a change in strategy," Uh-huh continues. "Are we not more likely to detect their propulsion, even if it is momentary, from a greater altitude?"

"Yes," Saucy allows, without changing course.

"Captain," Uh-huh says. "Please gain altitude. Ten iksiks, perhaps? And maintain a holding pattern. And set sensors to maximum sensitivity."

The creator of Oily understands the limitations of copyright protections, particularly as they relate to the ill-defined subject of literary and cultural influence. The creator of Oily understands the possibility that he himself may have been influenced during the production of the text; however, the creator of Oily understands that influences are impossible to pinpoint, and in the event that influences are pinpointed, the creator of Oily shall not be held liable. The only identifiable influence of which the creator is aware is an archaic European tale whose origins are murky and which has been in the public domain for centuries; its influence is limited to a relatively brief passage, reproduced in full below in order to avoid confusion:

Warren pulls the pie from the old electric stove and sets it on a rack to cool, ignoring the steaming purple fluid that drips onto the counter. "Smells good!" Penny calls from the bedroom, and he goes to see her.

"It'll run all over if I cut it now," he says. "I thought I might take a walk while it cools."

It only takes a moment, both of them calculating her need for his presence against his need for a quiet break. Before he can say, "Actually, I think I'll work on that novel I started last year," she says, "Go ahead. I was just about to take a nap."

And so Warren walks out onto the levee. A smell haunts the air. At first he thinks one of the neighbors has used too much lighter fluid in firing up the grill, but two blocks away he still smells it. Maybe a crew from the Department of Public Works has been filling potholes with hot asphalt a couple of streets over. He forgets about it until he takes a seat on the levee to watch an egret fish for its dinner. The smell is still strong, and he wonders if one of the chemical plants or oil refineries up- or down-river has released something nasty or maybe even exploded, because the smell has a smoky edge, and then of course he remembers the rig out in the Gulf, still burning. But it couldn't be that, could it?

While Warren is gone, a bit of commotion erupts in the bathroom. Penny thinks she hears water sloshing in there as she drifts off to sleep, but she doesn't stir. If she stayed awake, she might hear the toilet lid bump down on the seat lightly, and if she went to investigate she would see the black acorn nosing about in the collection of containers on the back of the toilet, finally tipping over a tin of bath salts that is just the right size and deftly maneuvering until the tin rests on the probe's back and it can navigate slowly through the bathroom door and make its way to the kitchen. If she rose at this point, she would assume she was still sleeping, for bath-salt tins only float in midair in dreams.

"Do you think we're safe?" Phthsspitty-snapp asks, after Jerry parks the probe and tin on the kitchen counter.

Jerry shuts down the probe and pops the exit hatch. "Not really," he says, unbuckling. "Maybe for a while." She follows him out onto the fuselage, and they both jump down to the smooth blue surface of the countertop. One corner of the tin rests on a thick square of fabric, allowing a little light in and leaving a gap they can roll under. "Do you smell that?" Jerry asks as they venture out into the open. "It smells like krkr-ha berries!"

With help from an electrical cord trailing from the radio sitting atop the breadbox, they are able to get up high enough to see the vast krkr-ha berry pie, all golden brown with pits of violet goo here and there. After eating nothing but reconstituted food on the mother ship and days of eating the Xxzzrrrvan equivalent of saw-dusty protein bars on the probe, neither of them hesitates to jump from the edge of the breadbox to the edge of the pie. They walk to the nearest opening in the crust, a seam along the edge where the filling has leaked out. First Jerry then Phthsspitty-snapp kneel to dredge a finger through the goo. "We really should analyze any native foodstuffs before ingesting them," Phthsspitty-snapp points out, but Jerry already has a mouthful. She shrugs and follows suit. They both roll their eyes, nodding.

"Not quite hot enough, though," Jerry says. "Maybe in the middle." And so they trek across the crust to the pie's center, where its maker has cut four vents. They kneel beside the nearest one, inhaling a berried steam.

"This part's too hot!" Phthsspitty-snapp says. She stands up, looking for crust openings between the center and the edge.

On his way back from the levee, Warren thinks of the aliens again, wishing they would come back but knowing it is unlikely, given the vastness of the world. He supposes he will either be one of those people who spends decades testifying to an unlikely alien encounter, or he will spend decades wondering about it and not telling anyone. If only he had kept the aliens captive and brought them to the university. Why didn't he? He always had an inkling that he was destined to claim some precious nugget of fame. It was why he wrote poetry in high school, why he had 73 pages of a novel stacked up in a corner of his study, why he threw himself into astronomy when he was sixteen, just knowing he could find a new comet that would be named after him, guaranteeing that the world would remember him every 80 or 130 years. And now those aliens are probably in someone else's Tupperware™ container, going to someone else's university, and someone else will be at the big news conference tomorrow. He didn't even take any pictures of them.

Someone has dripped water on the floor of the bathroom and knocked stuff off the back of the toilet—a little Q-tip™ box and a big can of shaving cream. Warren frowns, then shrugs and puts things back the way they were. He looks in on Penny, who lies on her side sleeping. In the kitchen he fixes himself some ice water before noticing that someone has been poking at his pie. Two toothpicks lie on the top crust, halfway between the edge and the center, their ends purpled, and a messy little hole has been poked through the crust. "Why would she...?" he mutters. When he bends closer and studies the pie, the little trail of violet dots from the hole to the edge almost looks like tiny footprints. The dots on the countertop are fainter, disappearing altogether after a few inches, but he notes their trajectory, which points toward three potholders that lie flat at the back of the counter. It looks like someone has been sleeping on the first one, and it looks like someone has been sleeping on the second one. It also looks like someone has been sleeping on the last one, and there they are—two little sideways aliens wearing silver jumpsuits. They are sprawled out on one corner of the potholder, eyes closed.

Jerry wakes up first, alerted by the warm, slightly rank breeze wafting out of Warren's nose. He sits up and stretches, then gives Phthsspitty-snapp a gentle shake. "Already?" she mutters.

"Why are you sleeping on my red potholder?" Warren asks.

"The orange one was too hard, and the blue one was too soft," Jerry would tell him, if he were dialed in to the probe's translator.

Users may or may not recognize the debt that the preceding passage owes to a certain fairy tale, whose rights at one time belonged to the Brothers Grimm and/or Mother Goose, but which under current copyright law is in the public domain. Even if the tale were protected by copyright, that copyright would not be violated by the preceding passage, which merely borrows certain structural elements from the tale (users will note that Goldilocks and/or her equivalent has been replaced by two aliens with indeterminate hair color/length, that there are but two "bears," and that the passage omits chairs and/or their equivalents). In addition, although certain users may recall that the song "The Distance©," written, performed, and copyrighted by the musical ensemble Cake™, contains the phrase "deftly maneuver," applicable copyright and trademark regulations do not require the creators and/or future publishers of Oily to secure permission for use of a brief phrase from a copyrighted song, unless the brief phrase is protected by its own trademark, as in the case of "Can't touch this™," which is not the case with "deftly maneuver."

Potential publishers of Oily shall note that the creator of Oily has covered all bases regarding trademark and copyright, indicating that Oily is "as close to ready for publication as possible," which is what writers have to do these days, as noted by many well-established literary agents such as Tanya Pueblo, who met with the creator of Oily in the summer of 2012.

VII. CREATOR RESPONSIBILITIES

A. Interactions with the Public: As creator of Oily, Warren Avon pledges to adhere to certain guidelines regarding his behavior (including but not limited to speech, gesture, facial expression, eating, drinking, and/or laughter) during interactions with the reading public, which includes but is not limited to readers, nonreaders, booksellers, passersby, pedestrians, emergency personnel, old ladies, young ladies, old men, young men, children, security guards, fellow writers, book reviewers, and/or heating, ventilation and air conditioning repairmen. Warren's behavior during all interactions with such personages (whether in-person, online, synchronous, asynchronous, by telephone, in public and/or in private) shall be cordial and/or non-rude, entertaining and/or non-boring, platonic and/or non-intimate, professional and/or non-unprofessional, and audible and/or non-inaudible. Warren's hygiene shall be compatible with community standards, and Warren shall refrain from wearing clothing that is provocative, smelly, garish, ugly, too big, too small, old, and/or stupid; no clothing shall display or otherwise include trademarked logos and/or slogans except those belonging to the clothing's providers and/or the publishers of Oily, should such publishers step forth in the future and pick up Oily for "real" publication.

Guidelines for specific interactions with the public:

> 1. Readings: From time to time, Warren may read portions of Oily aloud before audiences. Whether such performances take place in bookstores, basketball arenas, at festivals, in private homes, and/or elsewhere, Warren shall not read the entire text of Oily to a single audience. Warren pledges to read an accessible excerpt of a length appropriate to circumstances. The following excerpt provides an example, its length in this case being appropriate to a bookstore reading/signing, i.e. brief enough to leave plenty of time for patrons to

purchase books and have them signed (Warren pledges to preface the excerpt with some prefatory remarks to the effect that he values the bookseller's invitation to read/sign, values the efforts of the audience [no matter how small] to attend the reading/signing in spite of bad traffic and/or inclement weather and/or pleasant weather and/or political instability). (In addition, Warren pledges to preface his recital of the following excerpt with a note on its context, e.g., "Okay, so Oily is about tiny little aliens who come back to Earth hundreds of millions of years after their ancestors seeded the planet with life so that it would eventually produce petroleum. I'll let that sink in for a minute, ha ha! So this alien named Jerry and his intern Phthsspitty-snapp have been zooming around the planet in this little probe that looks like a long black acorn about the size of a fountain pen, and they're upset to find this human species using up all of the petroleum because they know their bosses will exterminate the species so that they can send the remaining petroleum back to their planet. Are you with me so far? Ha ha ha. So anyway, in this scene Jerry and Phthsspitty-snapp, who have sort of gone maverick, have taken refuge in Warren's house in New Orleans, because another alien probe has been chasing them and shooting at them because they think they're sabotaging the expedition, because Jerry drilled into an offshore oil well and caused it to blow up"):

"Where's your little spaceship?" Warren asks, and the tiny alien man stands up.

"Shh kkrr chk shh frr pip," the alien says.

"We need the translator," Phthsspitty-snapp points out.

"Hang on," Jerry says, and he holds up one finger to the alien giant, making the intergalactic signal for "just a minute." He runs across the counter and scrambles under the corner of the bath salts tin. He boards the probe and powers it up. While he waits for all of the systems to reboot, he sees light breaking into the open hatch behind him. Video comes up, and he can see that the alien has lifted one edge of the tin up high. One big eye, white with a brown and black center, peers in. "Come on," Jerry says, tapping on the console impatiently. *Downloading,* the console replies. At last it is ready, and he slides the portable broadcast translator out of its compartment by his feet. He manages to pin the microphone to his collar and the speaker to his sleeve as he scrambles for the hatch, and once he has emerged he shouts to the alien. "Please don't do that!"

What Warren hears is, "Kindly refrain from such conduct." Startled, he lifts his head from the counter and carefully lays the bath salts tin back down.

Jerry hurries over to Phthsspitty-snapp, jamming an earpiece into his ear and handing one to her.

Warren stacks his fists on the edge of the counter and balances his chin on top, studying the little aliens. He tries to imagine the threadlike bones in their tiny fingers. They look just like little people when they stand still, little people standing with their feet turned sideways, looking over one shoulder, like little people striking a pose before breaking into a neatly choreographed dance routine. "We require your assistance," the male one announces.

"Mine?" Warren says. "Really? Okay, okay. Just tell me what I can do."

"You must halt all use of petroleum on your planet," the alien says. "Else our government shall annihilate every member of your species."

Warren stands up, frowning. "Wait. Seriously?"

"I think that sounded like a threat," Phthsspitty-snapp tells Jerry.

"Shoot," he says, one hand over the mic. "This is why I never joined the diplomatic corps." He clears his throat, stepping forward. He speaks plainly, not realizing that the translator has mastered English since its last use and has a tendency to formalize his speech. "Allow me to explicate. My companion and I wish to save your species," it says. "From our government."

"Wow. And you want my help? Okay, so...does your government know about this?"

"Negative."

"Can your government really annihilate my species?"

"Affirmative."

"I'm not really in a position to tell the entire planet to stop using petroleum," Warren says. "But we can go to the media. This'll be huge. Wow." He feels light and wobbly, the way people feel when their dreams come true.

"But our government's protocols dictate that any species scheduled for elimination receive no advance notification of its imminent extinction. I fear that publicity would trigger an immediate launch of extinction packets."

"Then I don't—how can we...?"

"Perhaps we can collaborate on a comprehensive plan," Jerry says.

"Warren?" Penny says, shuffling through the doorway in her bathrobe. "Who are you talking to?"

"Talking to? Me?" Warren begins, but Penny is already squinting at the aliens on the counter. She bends at the waist, moving forward until her face is just a foot from Jerry and Phthsspitty-snapp, who stand calmly on the red potholder.

"Who are you?" she asks.

"I am Jerry," Jerry announces. "My companion is Phthsspitty-snapp."

"They're aliens," Warren offers.

"Right," Penny says. "Wow. Okay." She straightens. "Do aliens like ginger tea?"

"Ginger tea?" Jerry says.

"Right. Tea is...we make tea by pouring hot water over dried leaves of certain plants, but ginger is a root. I guess tea is any beverage made by soaking plant matter in—except for coffee. If you soak the roasted seeds of a certain plant in hot water, it's called coffee, but any other plant matter makes tea. Right, Penny?"

Penny is already chopping up a hunk of ginger root. "I guess so."

"You're not dreaming, by the way," Warren offers.

"Okay."

"That black acorn thing? That was their little spaceship."

"Okay."

"Penny's my wife," Warren explains. "She's a female, and I'm a male. We met eight years ago in college, which is an optional educational institution for adults, but most people do enroll in college—well, more than half, I think—after finishing twelve, I mean thirteen years of mandatory education from age five until age eighteen. But anyway...six years ago Penny and I got married, which means that we scheduled a government-sanctioned ritual that made us into partners but also served as a public declaration of our love and our intention to remain partners no matter what for the rest of our lives. Although it is possible to dissolve the partnership through 'divorce.' Not that we would ever do that. Nope. Never. We promised each other we would stay together forever, no matter what happened, and that's what we're doing."

"I see." Jerry says.

"And we really have a deep connection," Warren says. "Like right now she's leaning against the counter with her arms crossed, giving me a look that I can tell means *Now that you've explained me to these aliens, how about you explain these aliens to me?*"

2. Book clubs: Users of Oily who encounter Warren at meetings of book clubs and/or book groups and/or reading groups can reasonably expect Warren to adhere to these guidelines for his behavior, which at all times shall be polite, welcoming, open, and good-natured. In the event that Warren is offered food and/or beverage, users can reasonably expect Warren to understand the recommendation to accept such offers; however, users should understand that Warren may politely decline such offers, wholly or in part, due to vegetarianism and/or partial vegetarianism, illness and/or partial illness, physician's instructions and/or recommendations, and/or food allergies. Users should also understand that Warren may wish to refrain from drinking alcoholic beverages to excess during interactions with any member(s) of the public; Warren likewise accepts an obligation to refrain from drinking to excess during interactions with any member(s) of the public. In sum, members and/or nonmembers of book/reading clubs/groups may reasonably expect interactions with Warren to resemble the following

(with the understanding that such interactions may vary considerably from the following):

Janet: All right, so welcome to the December meeting of the Bisbee Public Library—are you—can we...? Okay. Okay. Thank you. Welcome to the December meeting of the Bisbee Public Library Contemporary Fiction Book Club. We are honored today to have with us the author of a new novel called Oily, and his name is Warren Avon. Welcome, Warren.

Warren: Thanks so much. It's great to be here.

Janet: Where's Hank? I thought he was going to come today. I saw him at the Safeway yesterday, and he said he was coming.

Chandler: It could be his wife. She's been sick lately.

Janet: Or I suppose he might be running late. Anyway, welcome, Warren.

Warren: Thank you.

Janet: Now of course we've all read Oily, and—

Jonathan: I'm only about halfway through, so no spoilers, please! Ha ha.

Janet: Well, Jonathan, I can't promise that, but I guess we could all say "Spoiler alert!" if we're about to give something away, and you could plug your ears.

Jonathan: I was going to finish it last night, but I had a beer with dinner and I just conked out before I could read two pages.

Janet: All right. Well, anyhow, Warren, I think one thing we'd all probably like to know is what inspired you to write a science fiction book? I know sci-fi is not your usual thing.

Warren: That's right, although I did read quite a bit of sci-fi when I was young—but no, you're right, sci-fi is not my thing. I had never written any sci-fi before. But actually I like to toy with ideas for movies and books that I never expect to write, just to say to my wife, "Someone should write a book called 'Heart of Brightness,' where a rainforest native travels from the depths of the jungle to the depths of an American city," or "They should make a movie called 'Crooks and Nannies,'" and years ago I came up with this idea for a sci-fi novel where aliens come to Earth and sort of shake their heads at all of the pollution and litter, and so it seems like these are environmentalist aliens or something, but it turns out they're upset because humans are wasting all of this petroleum that the aliens feel belong to them.

Gary: Spoiler alert!

Warren: Oh, did you—I don't know how far you've gotten, but that comes out pretty early on.

Jonathan: Yeah, no, don't worry. I knew about that. I just don't know how it turns out. Though I'm sure the good guys win.

Warren: Well, yes, they do.

Janet: And so one day you decided to write this book? Had you run out of ideas for books and this was all you had?

Warren: No, actually I had a few ideas for books—including "Heart of Brightness," which I've actually just finished, and I sure hope traditional book publishers snap it right up—but a couple of things inspired me to do this one. Of course, one of them was the British Petroleum® aka BP™ oil spill in the summer of 2010, which was fouling the waters of my adopted home state—

Janet: So you're not from Louisiana originally?

Warren: No, but I've lived there most of my life, and—

Gary: I didn't think so, because you don't talk like most of them talk down there. I worked for Shell ® back in the '80s, and they sent me down there once in a while. You ever heard of Norco? You know where that is? They've got a refinery there on the river, and we used to go down there for different things.

Warren: I do know where that is, and that is extremely interesting, sir! I hope we'll have a chance to talk afterwards!

Gary: Of course, back then they didn't drill in deep water because they just didn't have the technology. Not yet, anyways. But we used to drive into New Orleans and go to this one restaurant, it was up on the lake—I mean right on the lake, like part of it extended out over the water. I forget what it was called, but they had real good seafood and things, you know.

Margaret: I wanted to talk about the part where they all cook up a plan to save the planet.

Janet: All right, well, I don't know if you were finished telling us what inspired you....

Warren: Right, the BP™ spill, as I said, which actually occurred when I was halfway through drafting a very different version of Oily—different, but still about the abuse of petroleum, aliens coming to claim their petroleum, and so on. I sat down to write the day the news broke about the rig explosion, and I thought, "Well, this changes things," and the longer it spewed oil into the Gulf, the more I realized I would have to completely change the plot of the novel. I didn't know at the time that I still had nine years to go before I'd be finished—

Margaret: Nine years? Have you always been a slow writer?

Warren: Slow...? I don't know if that's especially slow. I mean, it is a long time to work on a novel, but plenty of other novels have taken longer. And I don't mean that it took me nine years to write 200 pages. That only took about a year, or maybe even less. No, it was the revising, looking for an agent, revising again, looking again...and somewhere in there, there was a period of two or three years where I was working on an equally excellent memoir (which, by the way, should be snapped up immediately by a traditional publisher), and Oily just sat in a drawer, untouched.

Margaret: Mr. Avon, I wanted to ask you about a scene in the middle of the book, where the aliens and Warren and Penny come up with a plan to save the planet.

Warren: Okay.

Margaret: Okay, it starts on page 122. Penny makes some ginger tea while Warren explains everything to her, she "...pours a little into a floral saucer and sets it on the breakfast table..." for the aliens to sip from, "...though for them it is somewhat like slurping tea from a kiddie pool..." and so on. Okay, here it is: Warren says, "How soon is your government likely to initiate this extermination?" And then "Jerry and Phthsspitty-snapp exchange a look. 'In approximately three days,' Jerry begins.

Warren and Penny widen their eyes at one another. 'That's—but—' Warren sputters. He notes a lack of despair in Penny's eyes. Has she already given up? he wonders, alarmed. He frowns thoughtfully, then sweeps his napkin to the floor and slides his tea mug out of the way. 'Here's what we'll do,' he says. 'We fly to New York. You two can just ride in my shirt pocket or something. We go to the United Nations. We're nobodies, though...but I guess if we show you to whoever, a security guard or receptionist, they'll take us right to their superiors, who'll take us to their superiors. Hopefully we can pretty quickly work our way up to someone important. The main thing is that we— you—request an emergency meeting of the UN and the president of the United States. Hopefully within a few hours they can draft a declaration saying that the whole planet will surrender its oil to your government. What's today, Tuesday? If we can get to New York tonight, convene the UN by tomorrow evening...hopefully there won't be too much squabbling, so by this time Thursday we can contact your government. Oh my God, this is just like the movies!'

Jerry bends down and takes an unhurried drink from the edge of the ginger puddle. 'I apologize,' he says. 'The Exploratory Board will act within three Xxzzrrrvan days, equivalent to approximately thirty Earth days.'" And then—well, there's more, but you get the idea.

Warren: You know, I think I know what you're going to say. As you're reading that, I'm realizing that I bought into the whole gender roles thing—Penny makes the tea, Warren takes charge. Why couldn't Warren have been the sick one? I should have made Jerry female and Phthsspitty-snapp male, not just to be PC and all that, but that would have been interesting. You know, writing is an endless process. Most writers say that they're never entirely satisfied with what they've written, that when they re-read it even after it's published they see things they wish they had changed.

Margaret: No, I was going to ask about the "lack of despair" in Penny's eyes. At the top of page 123? Shouldn't that be "look of despair"?

Jonathan: And why is the main character also named Warren? I thought this was a novel. Is it a novel?

Gary: Fitzgerald's! It was called Fitzgerald's!

3. Aspiring Writers: As creator of Oily, Warren pledges to refrain from becoming over-confident, arrogant, and/or cocky as a result of whatever success and/or accolades Oily garners. Warren further pledges not to respond with a bored and/or impatient and/or dismissive expression and/or utterance when approached by any person(s), whether in classrooms, at conferences, at parties, on large boats, and/or anywhere else. Moreover,

Warren understands the likelihood of contact with aspiring writers and the need to interact with such writers in an appropriate manner (aspiring writers are defined as children; grade school, high school, college, and/or graduate students; senior citizens; middle-aged citizens; blue-collar workers; unemployed individuals; and/or others who self-identify as writers and have written and/or intended to write poetry and/or fiction and/or nonfiction and/or texts of indeterminate genre with the intention and/or hope of reaching an audience, no matter how much and/or how little [if any] they have written, no matter how much or how little writing instruction [if any] they have received, no matter how much and/or how little [if any] of their work has been published and/or self-published and/or attempted to publish). Interactions with aspiring writers by Warren shall in all cases be positive and courteous, keeping in mind the notion that writing can be freeing and/or therapeutic and/or fun and/or gratifying and/or fulfilling and/or intoxicating and that it is not a competitive pursuit whose only goals are fame and/or fortune and that assembling words on an electronic and/or paper surface is in itself an accomplishment and that all persons should be welcomed to and encouraged in the creation of expressive and/or personally significant texts. These declarations, however, are not meant to imply that Warren has an obligation to assist any or all aspiring writers in developing their skills, finishing any texts, and/or publishing their work; any such efforts by Warren are evaluated on a case-by-case basis.

The following scenarios are fictional. Any resemblance to actual events in the past, present, or future or to persons living or dead (with the exception of Warren Avon) is strictly coincidental. Furthermore, the purpose of the scenarios is merely to demonstrate possibilities; they do not constitute a contractual obligation of any kind.

Minimal interaction:

Aspiring Writer: I loved your book.

Warren: Oh, thank you! Who shall I make this out to?

Aspiring Writer: To Tracy, please.

Warren: All right, Tracy.

Tracy: There was a lot of dialogue, I noticed.

Warren: Yes, I suppose there was.

Tracy: But it was great! I wish I was better at writing dialogue.

Warren: Oh, you're a writer, too?

Tracy: I'm working on a novel.

Warren: That's wonderful. Here you go.

Maximal interaction:

Aspiring Writer: I loved your book.

Warren: Oh, thank you! Who shall I make this out to?

Aspiring Writer: To Tracy, please.

Warren: All right, Tracy.

Tracy: There was a lot of dialogue, I noticed.

Warren: Yes, I suppose there was.

Tracy: But it was great! I wish I was better at writing dialogue.

Warren: Oh, you're a writer too?

Tracy: I'm working on a novel.

Warren: That's wonderful. Here you go.

Tracy: How do you do it? Any advice?

Warren: For dialogue?

Tracy: Yes.

Warren: Well, I guess I remember what an agent taught me. Her name was Tanya Pueblo, and she read the first chapter of Oily at a conference and then had a meeting with me. She told me I wrote good dialogue, which was flattering of course, but then she said, "You seem to realize that in good dialogue there's always some tension between the characters," which just crystallized things for me and helped me to really hone the dialogue.

Tracy: Tension?

Warren: Yes, like the characters don't quite see things the same way.

Tracy: Like they're arguing?

Warren: Not necessarily. It could just be that they don't understand one another, or their viewpoints are different. If all they do is agree with one another, it's boring.

Tracy: I guess I—I'm not—

Warren: Why don't you have a seat? I'll show you what I mean. Like right here, see? This is the part where Warren and Penny are talking to the aliens about what to do.

Tracy: Okay.

Warren: Let me just read this for a sec *...Jerry shakes ginger tea from his hands and then looks up at Warren and Penny. "We would prefer to enact a more organic solution," he says, his voice emerging tinny and bit squeaky from the speaker on his front shoulder.*
"Thirty days," Warren muses, glancing at Penny.
. *"We would like to keep our existence secret from all earthlings," Jerry continues. "Except for the two of you."*

"That's going to make it a lot harder," Penny points out. "People have been trying to convince the powers that be to cut back on oil for a long time."

"Maybe if you demonstrated your weaponry somehow," Warren says. "Or I could say that I invented whatever death ray you guys use. We'll blow up a mountain with it or something, and I'll pose as a mad-scientist-slash-criminal-mastermind, go on TV and demand that all petroleum production be halted. Not that I really want to be the world's all-time greatest villain."

"Our weaponry is limited," Jerry begins, shaking his tiny head.

Phthsspitty-snapp reaches out a hand, not quite touching his elbow. "Tell them about the prrbl," she says quietly.

"Then how can you wipe out our species?" Warren asks.

"What do I tell them?" Jerry asks.

Phthsspitty-snapp closes her eyes briefly, smoothing the front of her jumpsuit. She clears her throat and takes a small step forward. "On our planet there is an animal called the prrbl," she announces. "In ancient times it was used to carry supplies on long treks through the desert and across mountain ranges. But the prrbl seemed to despise its role and often refused to move or moved in the wrong direction—"

"Just like a mule!" Penny says. "We have mules and donkeys that fulfill the exact same role. Or used to."

Phthsspitty-snapp smiles. "Many planets do. And some prrbl-masters' solution was to prod, poke, or strike the prrbl, but they often found the prrbl responded by scratching them or scampering off into inaccessible ravines. Others tried luring the prrbl forward with tasty morsels—"

"The carrot-and-stick thing," Penny says.

"—But the prrbl ignored them. The best solution was to deceive a prrbl into believing it had decided of its own accord to move in the correct direction. Many props and optical devices were developed for the sole purpose of motivating prrbls."

"How about we take you guys to the White House?" Warren says. "Couldn't you reveal yourselves to just one more person?"

Penny waves her hand at Warren. "No, she's saying we have to make the powers that be think it's their idea to stop using oil."

"We have some hope that we could convince our government to delay extermination if we could show that your technology limits your ability to extract oil from beneath deep ocean waters," Jerry says.

"Well, I don't know if you watch the news or whatever, but a deep water oil rig not too far from here just exploded last night," Penny says.

"Yes, we are aware of it," Jerry says. "And we regret the deaths we caused. But if—"

Warren sits up. "You caused? Wait—"

Jerry freezes, wary. Phthsspitty-snapp doesn't seem to notice Warren's stiffening. She steps to the side and kneels to have another sip of the earthlings' fragrant tea. Jerry watches Warren's giant hands, ready to dodge to the right and leap off the edge of the table if he decides to slap them like insects. "The deaths were not anticipated," he says.

"No, I know," Warren says. "But you did that on purpose?"

"Yes," Jerry replies, relaxing as Warren slumps back in his chair again. "And a few such incidents within a short period of time may convince your powers-that-be to halt oceanic extraction, which may convince our government to postpone or perhaps cancel your species' extermination."

Warren studies Penny, who studies him back. "Worth a try..." he murmurs.

"Hell yes," Penny says. "Let's do it."

Tracy: I see! The tension, as you call it, is shifting and various, but ever-present.

Warren: Yes. The tension is subtle. It need not be exaggerated. At times it arises from slight misunderstandings, at times from minor disagreements, at times from differences in viewpoint. Despite the fact that this scene results in four characters agreeing upon a plan, the dialogue emphasizes the differences between the characters.

Tracy: Thank you Warren Avon, author of Oily. I will now return to my home and revise the dialogue within a short story upon which I am working, and as a result I shall find greater success. It is my opinion that your work should be promoted to a much wider audience, considering its quality and the quality of your interactions with aspiring writers such as myself.

Warren: You are too kind! I wish you well.

4. Accomplished Writers: As creator of Oily, Warren vows to refrain from becoming tentative, wary, timid, discouraged, and/or unproductive, no matter what criticism and/or lack of interest and/or lack of sales are generated by the publication of Oily, keeping in mind the knowledge that many writers have labored in obscurity without agents for decades before being discovered by wider audiences. Warren pledges not to respond with an obsequious and/or eager and/or puppy-dog expression and/or utterance when approached by any person(s), whether in

classrooms, at conferences, at parties, in his home, and/or anywhere else. Moreover, Warren understands the likelihood of contact with accomplished writers and the need to interact with such writers in an appropriate manner (accomplished writers are defined as professors, celebrities, novelists, psychologists, poets, journalists, and/or others whose success in writing and/or selling fiction and/or poetry and/or nonfiction and/or texts of indeterminate genre equals or exceeds the success of the creator of Oily by any measure). Interactions with accomplished writers by Warren shall in all cases be positive and courteous, keeping in mind the notion that publication and/or sales are not the only measures of success and that writing can be freeing and/or therapeutic and/or fun and/or gratifying and/or fulfilling and/or intoxicating and that it is not a competitive pursuit whose only goals are fame and/or fortune and that assembling words on an electronic and/or paper surface is in itself an accomplishment and that all persons should be welcomed to and encouraged in the creation of expressive and/or personally significant texts. These declarations, however, are not meant to imply that accomplished writers have an obligation to assist Warren in reaching users and/or buyers and/or sellers of Oily or conceiving and/or writing and/or revising and/or editing and/or publishing Warren's work; any such efforts by accomplished writers are pursued and conducted solely at their own discretion.

The following scenario is fictional. Any resemblance to actual events in the past, present, or future or to persons living or dead (with the exception of Warren Avon) is strictly coincidental. Furthermore, the purpose of the scenario is merely to demonstrate possibilities; it does not constitute a contractual obligation by any person(s).

Accomplished Writer: What's the name of your book again?

Warren Avon: Oily.

Accomplished Writer: Early? I think I saw that in *Publisher's Weekly*™ a while back.

Warren Avon: No, <u>Oily</u>.

Accomplished Writer: Nancy! What time are we going to dinner?

5. Attractive Women: As creator of Oily, Warren Avon understands the possibility that he may encounter attractive women in the course of promoting and/or discussing Oily and/or in the course of being the creator of Oily. Attractive women are defined as adult females whose faces and/or bodies and/or hair and/or clothing and/or speech is aesthetically and/or viscerally and/or otherwise pleasing. Warren Avon understands that

he may encounter attractive female readers and/or nonreaders and/or booksellers and/or writers and/or passersby and/or students and/or educators and/or hotel employees and/or others, and he understands and accepts his obligation to interact with such women exactly as he would interact with anyone else, i.e. politely and platonically. Attractive women shall not be assumed to expect and/or offer any form of special treatment from or to Warren Avon and shall not receive or offer any form of special treatment, intentionally or unintentionally. Warren Avon declares that he shall redirect attention to Oily in the event that an attractive woman evidently expects and/or desires any form of special treatment, as demonstrated in the following scenario, which is fictional. Any resemblance to actual events in the past, present or future or to persons living or dead (with the exception of Warren Avon) is strictly coincidental. Furthermore, the purpose of the scenario is merely to demonstrate possibilities; it does not constitute a contractual obligation by any person(s).

Warren Avon: Going down? Oh, it's you.

Woman with black hair and just a few freckles across her cheeks and nose: Oh, hey. Warren Avon. You headed out?

Warren Avon: I don't know. I thought I'd walk around a little, maybe see a bit of the city. The conference has been taking up all of my time.

Woman with black hair, just a few freckles, and shapely eyes: Tell me about it. That famous novelist and I are going to this cool tavern down by the river, if you want to join us....

Warren Avon: Oh, I don't know, ha ha. I've got—I should...I think I'm going to mostly do some work on revising Oily, you know, tightening up the language and all, like you suggested when we met one-on-one.

Woman with black hair, just a few freckles, shapely eyes, and small golden hoops in her ears: Fair enough. But if you change your mind, it's called Freddy's. The front desk can tell you how to get there.

Warren Avon: Sure thing, although I'll probably just work on the manuscript and give my wife a call.

Woman: Right. Well, I'm looking forward to reading the rest of your book, like I said.

Warren Avon: Yes...thank you. I'll send it to you as soon as it's ready.

Woman: And when *you're* ready. Like I was saying in the talk I gave.

Warren Avon: Right, because agents and editors are looking not just for promising manuscripts, but also for promising writers, writers who understand the whole process.

Woman: That's it. You have my card, right? Any my private email is tanyapueblo@litagency.com. All right. Bye.

NOTE: The limitations expressed herein do not apply to Warren Avon's spouse, despite her status as an attractive woman. Warren Avon's spouse shall enjoy special treatment, including but not limited to access to the text of Oily in manuscript form; special consultations regarding pre-publication decisions such as back-cover blurbs and front-cover design for print-on-demand publication; access to the private and/or non-public opinions, contemplations, musings, worries, and/or random thoughts of Warren Avon; rides in Warren Avon's car; and all public and/or private displays of Warren Avon's affection.

B. Provision of Backstory: As part of the efforts to create the illusion that characters appearing within Oily have depth and complexity, the creator of Oily shall provide backstory on principal figures within the narrative. Backstory is defined as information and/or details and/or scenarios and/or narrative fragments relating to and/or situated in the past (relative to the time frame in which the principal narrative occurs), with the purpose of adding depth of character (see Article IV). As user of Oily, you understand that in spite of the provision of backstory, it is unreasonable to expect that every and all possible pieces of information about principal characters be provided and that as user of a work of imaginative literature, you must engage and/or utilize your own imagination to a certain extent (see Article V).

Furthermore, as user of Oily you accept the fact that backstory may be intermittently interlarded within the narrative of the text of Oily and shall not be labeled, announced, or otherwise identified by headings, asterisks, special shading, embossing, or any other device and/or notation.

> 1. Jerry: Backstory on Jerry shall include but is not limited to the passage in which he recalls a scene on Bonruntun (see Article V) as well as a passage in which Jerry and another young first-year happen to come up to a table with two empty seats at the same time, both gesturing to the two first-years already starting to eat, making that vague this-seat-appears-to-be-empty-would-you-mind-if-I-sat-here face. The other two nod, chewing, and Jerry and the other fellow join them. "I'm thinking of going into navigation," one of the first two says. "What about you?"

"Analysis," the other guys says.

The first guy nods, turns politely to Jerry. "Have you chosen a concentration?"

Jerry nods. "Exploration."

"Ah, you want to get down on the ground. You got in already?"

"Well, I took the tests, and I think I did all right. We'll see."

The other fellow is willowy, maybe a little aloof, busying himself with chopping his steak tar-tar into precise chunks. "And how about you?" Jerry asks politely.

The willowy guy glances at all three of them with a shy smile. "Administration," he says, intoning the word as if it were slightly holy. "I got a 47 on the intake test."

"Wow, that's great," Jerry says, and the others nod, dutifully impressed. "Anyone else have Prappzik for Galactic History?"

"But I was first in my class at Xxarvard," the willowy one continues. He seems amazed rather than immodest, as if reciting startling facts about extinct animals. "And I got a 19 on my XXAT."

"I don't even remember what I got on my XXAT," Jerry laughs, and the others join in. The willowy one frowns. "I'm Jerry," Jerry says, extending his front hand to all three of them. Years later, he will be unable to remember the names the first two offer as they shake his hand, but he will still see the uncomfortable look on the willowy one's face before he finally looks up. "I'm Hmmm," he says, and goes back to his steak. Jerry makes a note to himself to avoid Hmmm, sensing that he will be aloof and despised for the duration of their course of study. He will mainly succeed in steering clear of Hmmm for the next two years, even managing to keep his name off of the petition that his classmates will circulate in the last semester and submit to the department chair to no avail. He'll do his best to forget Hmmm after graduation, but eleven years later he'll see him again. This time he'll be at the other end of a polished table in a narrow, brightly lit room. "The Committee finds your actions during the expedition to Botruntun reprehensible," he'll intone haughtily. "You are suspended." Years later, he'll surface again on the council that reinstates Jerry under probation, then attend the briefings before the expedition to Grawgraw, arriving late with his assistant every time. *Note to self:* Jerry will scrawl in the margins of the first meeting's agenda. *Steer clear of Councilor Hmmm.*

2. Phthsspitty-snapp: Backstory on Phthsspitty-snapp shall include but is not limited to disclosure of the fact that on the very day of Jerry's graduation from the Institute, Phthsspitty-snapp wakes up earlier than necessary, so that by the time her mother comes down the plastic stairs, she has already brushed her hair, put on the outfit they agreed upon the night before, and eaten her bitumen toast. An interminable half-hour later, the two of them walk out the door, leaving Phthsspitty-snapp's father and brothers to fend for themselves for the day.

They walk to the vertical transporter and take it to Level 42, where they catch a horizontal transporter to Sector 55732-A. As the transporters speed through their tubes, she looks out the window, again thinking about how Xxzzrrrva's shell of white honeycombed plastic is like the skin of a pitutu fruit, of how cell homes and cell stores and cell transporter stations would crack open if a giant decided to peel her planet, desks falling out of cell schools and businessmen falling out of cell offices on every continent. And underneath the thick white peel would be dark soil and rock. She has of course seen soil and rock on field trips to greenhouses and museums, but way down there is wild soil, mixed in with rock and tiny creatures she can hardly imagine.

"Almost there," her mother says happily, and soon they stand up to wait at the door as the transporter brakes to a stop.

Of course the zoo has farm animals, and even that is interesting because she has never seen a live prrbl, and it has been a couple of years since the field trip to the livestock farm, so she doesn't mind looking at skeerus and tricky-raws for a few minutes. She finds the wild animals more interesting, though it has been hundreds of years since anyone saw chuckos, smoors, or gollies in the wild, especially since there is no "wild" any more on Xxzzrrrva.

The center of the zoo is a dark building labeled "other." The air inside feels damp. Glass-fronted chambers line the walls, each a living diorama of life elsewhere, populated by exotic alien plants and lit by bulbs the color of alien suns. Her mother paces through quickly, giving all of them an appreciative glance, then moves towards the exit. Phthsspitty-snapp presses her face against each window, absorbing every detail. Something furry with teeth scrabbles through the grass at the back of the Botruntun exhibit, and colorful eels swirl under the surface of a deep puddle on Ti. She has to wait a minute to get to the glass of the Globard exhibit. Other children and a few parents stand in her way, peering intently at something big and green in the back corner. "Did it move?" one of the boys asks. "I think it moved a little." His father shrugs and pulls him away. Phthsspitty-snapp takes his place. The green thing looks like a pile of giant thorny cucumbers, and she scoffs internally at the boy who thought something moved, but then the pile shifts. She sees that four of the cucumbers are legs and the biggest is a body. Small yellow eyes wink open on the rounded head and a mouth yawns, revealing thorny white teeth. The sight electrifies Phthsspitty-snapp. She watches the cactus-dog sleep for another ten minutes, then runs to find her mother, to tell her what she has seen and what she will do when she grows up.

3. Warren: Backstory on Warren shall include but is not limited to description of his boyhood desire of *uncorking a booming kick.* Little Warren wants to *boot it sky-high.* And so he finds a football in the garage and carries it down the street to the grassy field where the high-tension wires pass through,

and he starts punting, telling himself and an imaginary audience that *to look at this kid you wouldn't think he belonged on a football field* and *his legs are skinny, but he's got perfect mechanics. They say it all began with a Sport Illustrated™ article on kicking when he was fifteen. He got his dad's old football out of the garage, blew the dust off it, and started kicking in a vacant lot down the street. His very first boot went forty yards.*

Warren holds the football just so, laces up, takes a few big steps, and steps into that first kick, which goes off the side of his foot and spirals clumsily into the azaleas at the edge of the Johnsons' yard. He revises the script as he trots after the ball: *His first kick went into the bushes, but he tried again, and...His first few kicks were nothing to write home about, but at least the third one went straight down the field, even if it didn't go very far, so he kept at it, and the next thing you knew, he—At first he could hardly kick the ball ten yards, but he was mighty determined. Every morning he did squat-thrusts or whatever in his bedroom, and every day after school he took that old ball—that old pigskin—down to the vacant lot to practice. His kicks got better, and before you knew it he was booming them sky-high. Everyone knows the rest of the story: that famous college coach happened to be driving by one evening, and he saw this kid uncorking booming kicks in a vacant lot. He stopped and watched for a while, then got out and told this kid he had to get on his high school football team, even though he was only a freshman, and that he would set records and in a few years he would come kick in college and set more records and be the highest-drafted punter in the history of the NFL draft and end up in the Hall of Fame. And he might turn out to be a great wide receiver, too.*

He keeps at it for a couple of weeks, spending an hour punting under the high-tension wires every day, adding details to the story and adjusting it as necessary. He hardly ever shanks it into the azaleas after a while, and some of his kicks go kind of high. His foot aches continually, because it is more like the ball is kicking him. And eventually he is discovered—not by a coach, but by stout eighth-grader Troy Johnson, who emerges from behind the azaleas one Thursday and starts pestering Warren. "Why are you always out here with that stupid football?" he asks. Warren just shrugs, internally adding a line about determination and perseverance to the story of his destiny. He kicks it nice and straight. Troy runs after it and scoops it up. "You suck," he says, and punts it back to Warren, only it goes way over Warren's head and bounces into the street behind him. Warren gets down on all fours to pull the ball out from under a Buick, then heads home. He puts the football away in the garage and goes upstairs to write in his journal, because *At one point he thought he would be a football player, but then he discovered poetry.*

4. Penny: Backstory on Penny shall include but is not limited to reflection upon the fact that someone famous once said, in some earlier century, that city and campus planners should not add sidewalks to public spaces until people have used the spaces for a year. In college Penny spends her junior year in a little apartment on the top floor of an old Victorian™ house at the edge of a vacant lot near campus. Students hurrying (or not hurrying) to class or hurrying (or not hurrying) home cut through the lot to get to the next street over and save a few minutes, and so an imperfect X of bare dirt paths crosses the grass. Whoever owns the lot fights a losing battle, posting Stay Off The Grass signs of increasing size and at one point

stringing the perimeter of the lot with yellow caution tape that gets stretched loose by people ducking under or stepping over it and then gets torn and then trampled.

Life on campus has a certain rhythm, and she finds she can count on seeing certain people at certain points as she goes through the week. On Mondays, Wednesdays, and Fridays she sees an extravagantly tattooed girl near the Chemistry Building as she hurries to Sociology 3345. On Tuesdays and Thursdays a slender young man will be crossing the field along one arm of the X as Penny crosses it along the other arm, and every day she sees a professor with a ratty briefcase and a pigeon-toed gait ambling along Seventh Street near Humanities. The kid who shuffles to class in slippers is liable to pop up in various places at various points.

"What are you doing?" she asks the slender young man one day. For the third time in a week, he has stopped near the hackberries in the corner of the lot and knelt down beside the path, picking at something in the grass. And so today she has left her path and walked across untrodden grass to get to him.

He stands up, embarrassed, then kneels down again. "There are these little gray and blue caterpillars in the grass," he says. "They get stepped on, so I'm moving them out of the way."

Penny does not understand the jolt of electricity that strikes her just then. "Really?" she says softly.

"In the fall you'll see a lot of little orange-and-black butterflies around here," he continues.

She just says "Wow," and he stands up, gives her an apologetic smile, and walks off. But she can't stop thinking about him—thinking no particular thoughts, but thinking—and the next day she speaks to him again and even helps him move a few caterpillars. On Monday she tells him she is Penny, and he says his name is Warren. The story continues the next day, and goes on for a long, long time after that.

VII. PROVIDER RESPONSIBILITIES

A. Potential Publishers: As editors, designers, manufacturers, advertisers, and wholesalers of Oily, any future publisher(s) who happen to step forth shall accept their obligation to provide a quality product. Quality relates to the following areas:

1. Correctness: As provider of Oily, any publisher shall possess final responsibility for the correcting of Oily. Initial responsibility rests with the creator of Oily, who shall provide digital text that is free of all major errors and contains very few if any minor errors. Any intentional and/or stylistic errors on the part of the creator of Oily shall be preserved in published versions of Oily. Any publisher may make appropriate efforts, in consultation with Warren Avon, to eliminate entirely all stray marks, improper apostrophes, misuses of than/then, pronoun case errors, sexist language, misspellings, etc. Users of Oily shall understand and appreciate any publisher's efforts in this regard, which are essentially invisible, i.e. successful editing and/or correction is not noticed, whereas failures to edit and/or correct are obvious and distracting, as demonstrated in the following excerpt, which is provided only for demonstration purposes and whose corrected/edited version appears in the actual text of Oily the product:

Phthsspitty-snapp crawls up the back of Penny's neck as the car speeds southwad. The stretch of smooth skin between the collar of Penny's sweatshirt and the edge of her hair proves challenging, and as Phthsspitty-snapp ressorts to digging her toes into Penny's skin and pinching hard with her fingers, she hopes Penny's bug-slapping reflexes will not take charge. At last she can grasp a handfull of hair and move upward more easily slithering herself through a dense forest of translucent brown strings until she crests Penny's cranium and stands in a little clearing formed by one end of her part.

"What do you think itll be?" Warren asks Jerry, who sits perched on his shoulder, gazing out at the onrushing road.

"I am not trained to speculate upon alien pathology," Jerry says gravely. "But fear not, for the probe's central processer shall provide a dependable diagnosis."

Phthsspitty-snapp kneels on Penny's scalp. She opens her back and picks up a nearby papery flake the size of a Xxzzrrrvan dinner plate. She stows it in the bag, then wraps both hands around a long hair and yanks it out, gathering it into springy loops, and shoves it in next tothe dead skin.

"Those are fishing boats," Warren says to Jerry, pointing at the vessels lining the broad bayou a long the road. "They voyage out into the sea via this bayou to capture small aquatic animals— well, some are large—with enormous nets. They bring back tons of the acquatic animals, mostly fish, but some crustaceans. Seafood processors by them and then prepare them by removing their shells or scales, maybe cutting them up, and then the processers sell them to restaraunts or stores, and then regular people buy them and eat them. But right now I think fishing in the Gulf is closed because of the oil spill."

"Our planet has no aquatic animals," Jerry says.

"Aren't there any oceans? There must be water."

"Their is water. Several oceans. But no aquatic life."

"How strange."

"One moment," Jerry says. "My colleague reports that she has gathered the necesary samples."

"What's her name again?"

"Phthsspitty-snapp."

"Pithity-snap."

"Phthsspitty-snapp."

"Ooh. Hello," Penny says, notising Phthsspitty-snapp's progress down her arm. "Now what do I do with this?" She lifts the bath salts-tin from her lap.

"Open the box and allow Phthsspitty-snapp to climb into it, "Jerry beguns, and a few minutes later Phthsspitty-snapp sits at the probe's control panel and the probe lays across Penny's palms, covered by the bath salts lid. "Take care to keep the shielding in place," Jerry cautions. "ANd momentarily you may feel a little—."

"Ouch!" Penny says. "Okay."

"I love this part," Warren says, as the car speeds up onto a high curving bridge, a ribbon of concrete that lifts them high enough to give them a veiw of the crumbling fingers of land all around them, the bayous and bays in between, and the open Gulf out in the distance before easing them back down to ground levle on Grand Isle.

"How long does the analysis take?" Penny asks, watching Phthsspitty-snapp squirm out from under the lid. She lifts her hand to Warren shoulder, and Phthsspitty-snapp jumps onto it, chattering at Jerry.

"Petroleum sensitivity," Jerry says.

"That's what I have?" Penny asks. Warren swears.

"According to our analisys," Jerry says.

Penny looks at Warren and he looks at her. It is one of those married-people looks, the kind that happens when both wish they could dismiss the world from their lives and be nothing but together. "Can you cure it?" Warren asks.

"Treatment is quit simple," says the squeaky voice, the little bug voice on his shoulder. "She must avoid petrolum and petroleum-derived products such as polymers, fuels, fabrics, cosmetics, medications, foods, and so on."

"Okay," Warren says thoughtfully. "But foods? I don't think we eat anything made of petroleum."

"Trace amounts in the crisp orange snack food you purchased at the fuel station," Jerry says.

"This is going to be hard," Warren says.

But Penny is smiling, shifting in her seatt to sit up a little higher. "Not really," she says. "I just need to make sure I wear cotton and stuff. No makeup. And lip balm—I'll make sure it has no petroleum gelly."

"And comes in a metal tin."

"Right! See? And I won't touch plastic," she says, and catches Warren's quick scan of the interior of the car. "I can get gloves—some thin coton gloves. Long sleeves. And no junk food. We usually don't put plastic in the microwave, but we'll have to make sure we don't store food in plastic or use plastic wrap. Organic shampoo."

"In a glass bottle?" Warren muses

2. Design: As creator of Oily, any publisher(s) shall accept their obligation to present the text of Oily in pleasing, readable form. Attention shall be paid to kerning, justification, spacing, and font design. As with editing, good design is invisible and under-appreciated. The following excerpt is kept short to spare users from prolonged exposure to harsh reading conditions created by poor design:

Penny stays in the car with the aliens while Warren goes into the convenience store with the Styrofoam™ bait boxes by the cash register. The little TV up high behind the counter is tuned to CNN™, and the top of the hour comes up as Warren waits to pay for his bottled water and Penny's glass bottle of tea. It is all deep voices and schematic animations, all "the flaming rig sank into the depths at 10:21 a.m. **central daylight time" and "Oil continues to spew from the compromised well" and "It is not known why the so-called blowout preventer failed." Warren doesn't notice when his turn comes up, and the deeply tanned cashier waves her hand at him. "Whatcha got, hon?" she asks. Warren snaps out of it and sets his purchases** on the counter. She smiles, glancing over her shoulder at the television. "This is worse than a hurricane," she says wryly.

"No doubt," Warren says.

When he gets back to the car he sees Jerry standing on the inside edge of the rear driver's side door. They wave at one another, and then Warren self-consciously inserts a *rectangular piece of polyvinyl chloride acetate with his name on it into the slot on a fuel-delivery device and inserts the fitting on the end of the fuel hose into* the side of his vehicle. "This car is relatively fuel-efficient," he says as he slides into the driver's seat a moment later. "The engine has four cylinders, which are…things inside the engine. A lot of vehicles have eight or six cylinders, and so they use more gas—gasoline. We call it 'gas,' even though it's a liquid—it's short for gasoline, which is stored in underground tanks beneath the pumps. Large trucks bring the gasoline to fuel stations like this one."

"I see," Jerry says.

"But you're wondering where the trucks get the gas! I never really thought about it. I suppose they come from refineries…but no, they probably come from storage facilities. They have these huge round metal tanks, above ground."

"But what is in your mouth?" Jerry asks. "You have chewed a bright green object continuously since you emerged from that small building."

"Oh! It's gum. Yeah, gum is...it's not food. It's sweet, very sweet, and flavored to taste like fruit or mint, which is a plant with a refreshing flavor. Gum is made of...something? I'm not sure what it's made of. But we chew it and it stays there—it doesn't break up or dissolve like regular food. So it gives you this flavor and sweetness, and I guess we like the act of chewing. Gosh, my mom grew up in a small town, and she said they used to dip their fingers in the vat of tar that a road crew would have, and they would chew the tar. Wow. I forgot about that. And I think traditional Inuits and other arctic peoples chew blubber in a similar way. So I guess it goes way back, but now we have this colorful stuff made of who-knows-what." He pinches one end of the wad of polyisobutylene gum and stretches it out. "Are we the weirdest species you've ever seen?"

"No," Jerry replies, but even filtered through the translator his voice sounded tentative.

3. Production Quality: Any publisher(s) of Oily shall accept their obligation to provide a durable product, free of significant physical flaws. Hardbound and softbound copies of Oily shall not have dog-ears, "ketchup" (stray ink marks), excess or insufficient binding glue, or dead bugs between pages, and shall be durable under normal reading conditions. Hardbound and trade paperback editions of Oily shall be constructed using acid-free papers, glue, and inks; mass-market paperback editions, if any, shall not. Although quality materials and production techniques generally ensure durability, no warranty, explicit or implicit, need be made regarding the term of Oily's resistance to wear and/or tear and/or abuse. No provision whatsoever need be made regarding repair or replacement in the event of humidity, aridity, infestation, exposure to the elements (including but not limited to earth, air, fire, and water), droppage, throwage, door stoppage, food and/or beverage spillage, and/or use as a wildflower preservation device. Keep out of reach of children under the age of 12, particularly those armed with crayons and/or markers.

Studies have shown that the page most likely to suffer damage due to user neglect and/or carelessness and/or abuse and/or downright cussedness is situated approximately two thirds of the way through any given book (excluding digital and audio books). As a precaution, the text of page 143 is displayed below, for use by users in the event of damage and/or loss for which users are wholly responsible, as in the case of spilling coffee when reaching for the telephone or dripping sulfuric acid during the construction of a robot:

the shade of the little house, which stands on five foot pilings. "Will they think it's weird that we're renting the house but sleeping out in the sand?" Penny says, eyeing the next camp, a turquoise number whose pilings must be sixteen feet high. "They might think we're squatters."

"We'll be going in to cook and use the bathroom and all," Warren says. "Or I will, at least. And you know what? If anyone asks, we'll just tell them about your allergy."

Warren takes off in the car to get supplies. While Penny sits on a low dune out behind the camp, looking out at the surf coming in off the Gulf, Jerry and Phthsspitty-snapp sit on her shoulder. Jerry clears his throat and turns up the volume on his translator, but Phthsspitty-snapp stops him before he can speak. "Not now," she says. And so all three of them study the waves, clouds, and sand.

Eventually Warren's car careens into the sand at the end of the driveway, and he hustles out to open the back door and trunk. Penny helps him unload a couple of big untreated canvas tarps, a coil of manila rope, glass bottles of apple juice, cardboard canisters of oatmeal, and

4. Advertising: Potential and future publisher(s) of Oily, if any, accept their obligation to produce promotional materials which appropriately convey the nature and spirit of the text of Oily. Any promotion in digital, audio, video, print, or other media shall be the responsibility of the publisher of Oily, although that responsibility does not preclude promotion in any media by any other person and/or entity. Users and others wishing to promote Oily on Facebook®, tee shirts, baseball caps, placards, magnetic automotive signs, and/or in conversations, classified advertising, and/or letters to the editors of periodicals shall be encouraged but not compensated, and users undertaking independent promotion of Oily shall understand their obligation to adhere to all laws, regulations, and stipulations regarding copyright and trademark (including but not limited to those mentioned in Article VI of this document). Examples of acceptable user promotion are provided below.

Facebook® posting and discussion:
Chris Doe is really enjoying Warren Avon's novel Oily™.
Pat Smith: Ooh, I've heard about that. Is it as good as they say?
Terry Johnson: I bought it but haven't started reading it yet.
Pat Smith: Get crackin'!
Chris Doe: I'm almost finished with it and yeah, it's good.

Kelly Scott: I love the part where they go looking for a charter boat to take them out to the oil spill. The main character wanders around the marina with his wife while the two tiny aliens hide in his collar, and he's like "We want to go out to the spill area," and all of these crusty Louisiana boat captains are like, "That's crazy. Leave us alone."

Chris Doe: They weren't all crusty.

Kelly Scott: You're right. Only a couple of them. That one guy was all slick and smooth, with his fancy sport boat and the shirt and hat with boating and fishing logos all over them.

Chris Doe: He was the one who said, "Get off my dock unless you want to go catch some state-record specks and reds." Or whatever.

Kelly Scott: Wasn't that the fried-chicken tycoon?

Chris Doe: No, the fried-chicken tycoon was friendly, remember? He's the one that wound up taking them out there. But first they went to where all the commercial fishing boats docked, but they were all loading up with absorbent boom and going out to string it along the coast.

Pat Smith: Is it too late to say "spoiler alert"?

Chris Doe: Oops. Sorry about that. At least we're not giving away the ending.

Kelly Scott: I loved the ending.

Chris Doe: Shh!

Web log ("blog") posting:

Well after last week's fiasco I don't know if I should even show my face online, but maybe it's blown over by now. I'll try to keep it positive. How about I tell you about this awesome novel I'm reading? It's called Oily. You've probably heard of it. It's by a guy named Warren Avon, who must be some kind of evil genius or something. Well maybe not an evil one...anyway the book is about these aliens who come to explore planet earth and they're upset at all of the pollution and plastic trash, but it turns out that's because they have come to harvest earth's petroleum and we've already used up most of it. The alien government decides to exterminate the human race, but two alien scientists kind of go rogue and hook up with this human couple to try to keep that from happening.

It's kind of a comedy and I love it! One of my favorites scenes happens when the rogue aliens and the human guy are riding out into the Gulf aboard this huge speedboat belonging to a fried chicken tycoon named Cope Allen. Although US copyright law only allows users to post an excerpt of 120 words or less in an online environment, I love this paragraph:

"The enormous green and orange bow pierces the waves, spray washing over the jaunty *Sinbad's Chicken* logo covering the foredeck. Despite the fat cushioning of the white leather cockpit, the ride rattles Warren's teeth, and with the roar of two huge ill-muffled engines there is nothing to do but look around. Sun glitters off of the waves on all sides, and white fishing boats dot the horizon. Warren studies Cope's happy profile for a moment, reflecting that Cope is the sort of guy who looks like Elvis without meaning to— happily overweight, lush black sideburns, and chunky sunglasses in a style Elvis would wear if he were still living. And he will be immortalized, Warren thinks, because this part will be in the news when the story all comes out, and in the books and movies people will write and make in the future. He gazes off at the horizon, at the same time picturing a muscular, handsome actor gazing off at the horizon, pretending to be him."

Isn't that awesome? By the way, they're on the Sinbad Special because Cope Allen was the only guy they could find who would agree to take them out to the site of a horrendous offshore oil spill, which is obviously modeled on the 2010 Deepwater Horizon™ catastrophe. I don't want to give too much away, but you won't believe the real reason behind the spill.

Well don't get me started. I could go on and on, but I won't. All of you should immediately purchase Oily at full retail from your local bookstore!

Post a comment:

Iglooman73@lol.com wrote: Yeah I finished reading it last week your'r right it is awesome and should be on every bestseller list and top 10 books list and should be made into a movie starring Jake Gyllenhall and that girl from Alice.

Classified advertisement:

Divorced guy on the cusp of 40, liberal, seeks like-minded unmarried gal for friendship that might evolve into something more. Love indie music, short walks on long beaches, and good novels like Warren Avon's *Oily*, for example.

Baseball cap text:

Oily
by

Amazon.com™ review:

Love this awesome book, August 11, 2019
by <u>Steven Johnson</u> - <u>See all my reviews</u>
First off, it's about time someone wrote a book like this. It's not the first comic sci-fi novel (see Douglas Adams, Terry Pratchett, etc.) and it is far from the first socially-conscious sci-fi novel, but it really is special, kind of a madcap story but one written with great care and even love. It's full of surprises--don't read it unless you love surprises. Obviously it's about oil, the environment, energy issues, and so on, but Avon's got a light touch and doesn't beat you over the head with the message. It's like a fable, but he lets you figure out the moral of the story for yourself.

Users and/or potential users and/or non-users of Oily should note that the above examples are provided free of all copyright and/or trademark limitations. Users and/or non-users may scan, copy, write down, and/or cut and paste text from the above samples without fear of litigation, prosecution, stigmatization, or saber-rattling.

B. Potential Booksellers: Although any potential publisher(s) of Oily shall provide a quality product, it is the sellers of Oily that shall have direct and/or indirect contact with users and/or potential users and/or non-users of Oily, and, as such, booksellers shall have certain duties and responsibilities relating to the provision of Oily to members of the public.

1. Bookstores: In the event of traditional publication of Oily by any traditional publisher with no help from Tanya Pueblo or her ilk, employees of retail bookstores large and small shall have special opportunities to orientate potential users of Oily to the product through face-to-face interactions before and during the point of sale. Proprietors, managers, employees, associates, sub-contracted employees and volunteers for retail bookstores shall accept their obligations to act as advocates for and promulgators of Oily in the course of conducting their duties. Advocacy for and promulgation of Oily need not exceed or supersede advocacy for and promulgation of other products; neither shall advocacy for and promulgation of any other product(s) exceed or supersede advocacy for and promulgation of Oily. Recommended actions shall include but not be limited to:

a. Placement of Oily among "Staff Favorites" (or Similar).

b. Face-Out Placement of Oily on Shelves.

c. Placement of Oily On Themed Display Tables: Examples include "New Releases," "Bestsellers," "Summer Reading," "Winter Reading," "Perfect Gifts," "Pulitzer™ Nominees," "You've Seen the Movie Now Read the Book," "School Reading,"

"Required Reading," Etc. Placement of Oily on sale tables ("Buy One, Get One Free," "Reduced," "Last Chance," "Remaindered Titles," "Cheap Crap," "Free") is discouraged.

d. Pleasant Momentary Interaction Regarding Oily: Store employees are hereby encouraged to insert brief point-of-sale comments such as "Good choice," "Love this book," "I've gotta read this," "I was thinking of buying this for my dad's birthday," or "epic win."

e. Pleasant Extended Interactions Regarding Oily: Should the opportunity arise, store employees are encouraged to invest time and effort in fulsome conversation(s) with bookstore patrons, perhaps modeling their behavior upon the following hypothetical dialogue:

Dan the employee: Finding everything all right?

Jan the customer: Actually, I could use some help.

Dan: That's what I'm here for. What's up?

Jan: I just have a hankering for some comical, socially-conscious science fiction, but I can't seem to find any.

Dan: Hmm. Let me think. Oh, I know. Follow me.

Jan: But sci-fi is right here.

Dan: Some of our sci-fi titles are in the literature section.

Jan: How long have you been working here? I haven't seen you before.

Dan: About a month. I worked at the Siegen Lane location for a couple of years before that. You must come here a lot.

Jan: Yes. Yes, I do.

Dan: Here we go. Take a look at this.

Jan: *Oily* by Warren Avon. Wow.

Dan: Yeah.

Jan: Love the cover.

Dan: I know, right?

Jan: So it's good?

Dan: It is good. It's funny, but in a thoughtful way, you know? It's hard to believe so many agents and editors passed on it. When he finally resorted to self-publishing, the world sat up and took notice.

Jan: But is it well written?

Dan: I think so. Avon is an excellent writer. And I hear he's very modest.

Jan: OMG, I forgot my reading glasses! I like to open up to a random page and read a bit before I choose a book, just to get a feel for it. I guess I could come back tomorrow.

Dan: Why don't I read to you?

Jan: What? No...really?

Dan: Sure. Why not? Let's just sit in two of these big comfortable chairs over here.

Jan: You're awfully sweet.

Dan: Aw, it's nothing. It's been a while since I read Oily, and I enjoyed it so much that reading a bit from it will be a real pleasure for me. Should I read the beginning?

Jan: No, just open it up to the middle and start reading. Writers are always on their best behavior on the first page, but I like to see what their workaday prose is like, see if they can maintain that first-page sparkle all the way through.

Dan: All right. Let's see. Ahem. Oh, this is the part where they're—

Jan: That's okay. You don't have to explain the context.

Dan: Okay. Here goes:

Jerry and Phthsspitty-snapp stay in the probe during the voyage out to the spill, having climbed inside before Warren boarded Cope's boat. Warren stowed the probe in the bath salts tin and carried it aboard as inconspicuously as possible, hoping Cope wouldn't ask what he was doing with the metal box with the stylized flapper girl on the lid. Soon Jerry and Phthsspitty-snapp heard the roaring engines and felt motion, which grow increasingly violent as the boat reaches open water and picks up speed. They strap in and sit at the control panel just to keep from bumping around, and Jerry powers up the probe. "What are you doing?" Phthsspitty-snapp asks.

Jerry shrugs, fiddling with a control orb. Within a few moments, the familiar voice of a certain CNN™ news anchor emerges from the overhead speakers. It takes Jerry a little longer to get the video feed up, but soon they are immersed in all of the latest information about their destination. "How much is one thousand barrels a day?" Jerry asks. "Calculate that for me, would you?"

Phthsspitty-snapp pulls up the Xxzzrrrvan-to-Grawgraw conversion utility on a small monitor to her left. "That's about 200 million oobalings per Xxzzrrrvan day," she says. "Wow."

Jerry shrugs again. "I wish it were more."

"Oh, but what a waste of petroleum," Phthsspitty-snapp says. "I mean, I know it's *their* petroleum, but think of all of the Xxzzrrrvan houses and schools that could be formed, and all of the transporters and personal vehicles that could be fueled...."

"And all of the space voyages to find more petroleum and wipe out more species," Jerry says, mimicking her tone.

"I know," she says. "But isn't it too late?"

Warren wishes Penny had come along, though of course a long afternoon aboard a twin-engine plastic behemoth would have sickened her more than anything. Before they parted he had caught her looking at him and given her a rueful smile, both of them knowing that later they'd find a chance to marvel over the fact that they were carrying around tiny space aliens and to puzzle out what had caused her more memorable flare-ups and to bemoan the difficulties of keeping her clear of petroleum products, to wrestle the conundrum of water—would it be better to drink tap water from a glass or distilled water from a plastic jug, or could they find a store that sold water in glass bottles? For the moment they could only look at one another, thinking the same things and promising themselves they would talk about it later.

> Jan: Ooh, I like that.
>
> Dan: I know, right?
>
> Jan: It's so kind of you to read to me like that. But I guess you do it all the time.
>
> Dan: Actually, that's the first time I read to a customer.

Jan: I'll bet your girlfriend loves it when you read to her.
Dan: Oh, I don't have a girlfriend.
Jan: I see....

C. Lenders: Special restrictions apply to institutions and individuals that lend copies of Oily to individuals. Lenders shall accept the fact that each use of a copy of Oily exacts a toll in terms of wear, tear, and disrepair, despite the fact that any publisher(s) of Oily shall manufacture a relatively durable product. Frequent lenders, whether institutional or individual, are encouraged to purchase multiple copies of Oily. Special restrictions are enumerated below.

1. Institutional Lenders: Libraries and other entities shall accept their obligation to catalog Oily as a work of fiction and to store any copy or copies of Oily where members of the public may find it or them. Libraries and other entities further accept their obligation to create and maintain accurate catalog records, recognizing the fact that cataloging errors (e.g., "Olly," "Waren Evon") may result in retrieval difficulties and consequent patron frustration. Libraries and other entities must not cover any copy of Oily in a pea-green library binding unless and until Oily has been out of print for a period of at least five (5) years. Furthermore, any institutional tags, stamps, stickers, and/or handwritten text must not obscure any part of the text of Oily, including but not limited to front and/or back cover copy, spine copy, and/or copy appearing on any internal page of Oily, including

front and/or back matter. The consequences of careless institutional tagging, stamping, stickering, and/or handwriting are briefly demonstrated here:

With the massive engines idling, the boat heaves and rocks gently but nauseatingly in the steely waves. Cope stands/leans at the helm, one buttock on the white leather captain's chair, poking at a color navigation screen in the dash. "I think it's to the west, maybe a few miles," he shouts.

"There're some boats over that way," Warren says.

"Wait." Cope peers at the screen, muttering. "No, it's to the east."

"That looks like a Coast Guard boat," Warren says, a bit louder this time.

"You hear about that dome thing?" Cope yells. "They're going to try putting this giant funnel device over the spill. It won't work."

The bath salts tin rattles like an old alarm clock. Warren turns away from Cope and cracks the lid to peer in. The probe noses through, hesitates, then flies overboard and pierces a wave.

"Won't they find us?" Phthsspitty-snapp asks, gripping the edge of the control panel as the probe speeds downward into darkening water.

2. Individual Lenders: Although at the time of this writing Oily was available as a free (gratis) e-book, the lending of published (print-on-demand and/or traditionally published) copies among individuals is discouraged. Although US copyright laws prohibit the prohibition of the lending and/or borrowing of single copies, users of Oily are hereby requested to deflect loan requests by friends, acquaintances,

relatives, neighbors, colleagues, classmates, fellow employees, strangers, employers, household servants, and others by suggesting individual (free) download or purchase through licensed retailers, not because the creator of Oily wishes to profit financially but because he wishes to be able to gauge the popularity of Oily. The creator of Oily seeks readers, not money; however, in the event of publication by any traditional publisher(s), users must understand that excessive lending diminishes the return on publisher(s)'s investment. The creator of Oily shall appreciate that investment and do his level best to make it worthwhile.

Lending to members of users' immediate family is permitted, provided such family members occupy the same household as the user. The request to deflect such requests is non-binding, as required by US copyright law. The following dialogues demonstrate conversational strategies for deflecting loan requests:

> a. User's Colleague: Say friend, I wonder if I might borrow your copy of that novel, Oily, so that I could read it for next Saturday's employee book club meeting?
> User: Yeah, the thing is I haven't finished reading it yet. Sorry, pal.
> User's Colleague: That's fine. Perhaps I will ask Marsha.
> User: Ooh, you don't want to do that. Marsha had that nasty cold last week, and

she was probably sneezing and coughing all over her copy.

User's Colleague: Gosh, you're right. Let me just check with David.

User: David? Wow. Yeah. I tried to borrow a sheet of paper from David during a meeting once, and he told me I was irresponsible for not having my own.

User's Colleague: Maybe Barbara....

User: I'm not sure, but I think Barbara probably quit the book group.

User's Colleague: Oh well, I guess I will purchase my own copy down at the bookstore.

User: Well, that's what I did, and I really think it's better that way. Then you have your own copy, and you can read it again in a few years and you don't have to worry about wrinkling a page or getting coffee on it since it belongs to you. And besides, if everyone just borrowed copies of books, the writers of books would miss out on potential earnings.

User's Colleague: All of this is true. I understand. Why did I think I wanted to borrow the book when I can purchase it myself? Considering the hours of entertainment that the book will provide, its cost is quite low compared to other forms of entertainment such as videos, movie tickets, and music albums.

Jerry lights the illuminators as the probe races deeper through dark water, flecks of organic matter, alive and dead, flashing across the monitor. As they near the seafloor, Phthsspitty-snapp gasps at the sight of an enormous writhing animal just ahead, but in a moment the probe passes through the animal, which is just a huge brown plume of petroleum and seawater.

The riser pipe lies crooked across the flat seafloor, oil billowing from its broken elbows. Jerry flies a lazy oval over the whole site, and Phthsspitty-snapp gets a glimpse of the sunken rig lying on its side in the murk, twisted and blackened. "What are we doing?" she whispers. "Aren't they going to find us now?"

"Possibly," Jerry says. "But I suspect they've returned to the mother ship, so the signal will be pretty weak, especially through all of this water."

"Still."

Jerry shrugs. "It'll take them a while." He steers for the ragged end of the riser pipe, avoiding the brown billows but moving in close. Several smaller tubes and pipes protrude from the pinched end, and the oil spews from the drill pipe. "This'll get their attention," he says. He arms the weapons system.

"What—" Phthsspitty-snapp begins, but he starts pulling the trigger, blasting the drill pipe here and there in short bursts until the end of it, pinched by the violent bending that broke it off, has enough new holes that the brown cloud of oil tripled in size.

"That's better," Jerry sighs, powering down the weapons system. "Now back to that noisy boat."

User's Colleague: Wow, yeah.

b. User's Employer: I see you're reading Oily. Let me borrow it when you're finished.
User: No.
User's Employer: If you do not let me borrow Oily when you are finished with it, I will fire you.
User: That's against the law, so if you make me lend you Oily when I am finished with it under threat of termination, I will notify the Equal Employment Opportunity Commission.
User's Employer: You are right. I do not know what I was thinking. I apologize, and I will purchase Oily from a bookstore on my way home from work tonight.
User: That's more like it.

c. User's Neighbor: Hey, good morning! I hope it's not too early for you, but...
User: No, no. Come on in. What's up?
User's Neighbor: You're not going to believe this, but I came to borrow a cup of sugar. Just like the old days! My son just got engaged, so we decided to have a little lunch party—just family and close friends—and I went to Albertson's yesterday and got everything I needed, but I didn't realize I was almost out of sugar, which I need for the banana-nut bread.

User: Oh, no problem! Come on.

User's Neighbor: I hope you weren't in the middle of something.

User: You know what, I was just sitting here reading. Dennis took the kids fishing, so I've got some time to myself.

User's Neighbor: Oily? What's that? Wait, I think I heard about it....

User: Yeah, it's this novel where tiny aliens cause the oil spill.

User's Neighbor: Right! My friend Andrea told me about that. She was going to lend it to me, but she'd already passed it on to one of her friends and she wasn't sure when she'd be getting it back.

User: It really is good. You should read it.

User's Neighbor: I'm kind of picky about novels, but it does sound good.

User: Here, listen to this. I was just reading it when you came over:

Cope's boat is easy to find. Jerry takes the probe up a few hundred feet and spots the bright green and orange craft bounding noisily through frothy brown waves to the southeast. He matches its speed and eases the probe down behind Warren, then slides around to his lap and knocks on the tin, startling Warren out of a reverie that involves composing a description of Cope suitable for the book he will write about the role he and Penny are playing in the alteration of human history for the next millennium, although he wonders whether it will be a desperately scratched-out scroll left behind as his species vanishes or the "authoritative, inspiring, and definitive account of a young couple's role in saving the human race from aliens, from petroleum, and ultimately from itself," which is what the back (or maybe the front) cover will say. He fumbles with the tin, holding it open once he gets a grip on it. Jerry parks the probe and shuts down most of the systems.

Warren stands up and makes his way forward, holding onto the seats to steady himself against the wind and the bounding motion. He pokes Cope's shoulder. "That's good, Mr. Allen. We can head back now."

"Seen enough?" Cope shouts, grinning. "It's an awful mess out here." He shakes his head and works the wheel and throttle, slowing to point the boat back toward the distant marina.

"What are you doing now?" Phthsspitty-snapp asks, trying to get a look at a small monitor on Jerry's side of the control panel and catching a glimpse of text jumping and flying across the screen.

"Hacking into a certain somebody's space mail," he says, fingers intent on the control orb. He pauses, leans forward. "Here it is: 'Councilor Hmmm: Having received your urgent communication regarding the distortion of mission objectives on Grawgraw-3, the Exploratory Board hereby approves independent management of the mission, provided whatever actions taken henceforth comply with Protocols 3.14-3.27. Please follow the accelerated report schedule outlined in section blah blah blah.' Figures."

"What does it mean?" Phthsspitty-snapp asks.

"Come on, you had a course in Exploratory Board protocols, didn't you?"

"It was part of the history course."

"Right. I guess they made some curriculum revisions." Jerry shakes his head.

"I think they did that so they could make room for the ethics course," Phthsspitty-snapp says. "Not that it did any good."

"Depends on how you look at it," Jerry points out. "What's more unethical, breaking the rules that allow us to exterminate alien species, or abiding by them?"

"Wow. Ouch."

Jerry laughs. "We can talk about it later. At any rate, the space-mail is saying Hmmm can decide for himself when to commence extermination. Listen to me—'commence extermination.' It means he can kill off this species as soon as he wants."

Phthsspitty-snapp slumps. "I guess that's it then. Nothing we can do."

> User's Neighbor: Pretty good.
>
> User: You see what I mean? The whole book is like that.
>
> User's Neighbor: I am going to take your advice and immediately purchase this book from a nearby bookstore!

> 3. Theft Victims: Users accept their obligation to guard against theft of their personal copies of Oily. The creator of Oily understands that not all theft is foreseeable and/or preventable, but the creator of Oily requests that users not leave Oily lying around in plain sight where it can easily be purloined by purloiners professional and/or amateur. Users are advised to bring Oily with them to the restrooms of coffee houses, restaurants, libraries, and/or other public places. Users are advised to tuck Oily under one corner of their beach towels before going for a

swim at a beach and/or pool. Users who carry Oily in purses and/or briefcases are advised to keep a firm grip on the straps and/or handles of their purses and/or briefcases.

IX. DISCLAIMER OF WARRANTIES

A. Material Warranties: The creator of Oily makes no guarantee and/or warranty regarding the physical integrity and/or durability of physical copies of Oily, whether they be the print-on-demand version or versions produced by future traditional publishers, if any. The creator of Oily makes every reasonable effort to ensure production of a durable product (see Article VIII). However, it is not possible to ensure that every single page of every single copy of Oily be free from defect. Users encountering manufacturing defects may or may not request refund or exchange from the retail outlet that provided their copy of Oily, depending on policies stated in future iterations of this TOU agreement.

B. Other Warranties: The creator of Oily makes no guarantee and/or warranty regarding the literary and/or monetary value of Oily. Users should understand and accept the fact that less than one tenth of one percent of novels increase in value after retail purchase. All other novels depreciate immediately and steeply, such that one year after purchase most novels retain but 25% of their value; this applies to signed and unsigned copies equally.

Furthermore, the creator of Oily believes that it has high literary value, but cannot guarantee that critics, Amazon reviewers, booksellers, casual acquaintances, museum security guards, and/or others will share that belief. Users should be prepared for a wide range of possibilities regarding marketplace and public perceptions of Oily. For example, users reading Oily on a beach may have experiences similar to the following scenarios:

Worst-case scenario:
Passerby: Whatcha reading?
User: Huh? Oh, it's this novel called Oily.
Passerby: Oh, I've heard about that. Is it as bad as they say it is?
User: Umm….
Passerby: Jason! Wait up!

Best-case Scenario:
Passerby: Whatcha reading?
User: Huh? Oh, it's this novel called Oily.
Passerby: OMG, where did you get that? I've been looking everywhere, trying to find a copy. The library has a six-month waiting list.
User: I got lucky and found one at the airport, stuck behind some muscle-car magazines.
Passerby: I'll give you twice what you paid for it.
User: No way.
Passerby: Three times.
User: Sorry. It's not for sale.
Passerby: Could I just borrow it? I could just sit here and read it while you go swimming or whatever.

User: I don't really know you.

Passerby: That's true. I understand. Maybe you could just read it aloud. You don't even have to start at the beginning. Just read aloud from the part you're reading right now, just for a few minutes. Please? I'm dying to hear a little bit of the prose, which one reviewer characterized as "sparkling and pungent."

User: Well...all right. Here goes: "Warren lies on his back in the dark, listening to the faint waves coming in off the nearly flat Gulf. Various bugs buzz and chirp from the clumps of grass scattered here and there in the sand. He hears another sound, a constant sort of scribbling he can't identify. 'You awake?' he asks, and Penny rearranges her body to face him, giving a little affirmative hum. 'What's that noise?'

Penny lifts her head and stays motionless for a moment. 'It sounds like...CNN™?'

Warren taps the lid of the bath salts tin nestled in the corner of the tent. 'Jerry? Hello?' There comes a scratch of static, then Jerry's mechanically rendered voice. 'Yes?'

'Could y'all turn the TV down a bit, please?'

'Yes, of course.'

'Thanks.'

'You're welcome.'

'So how are you?' Warren asks Penny.

'About the same. I think it'll take a while.'

He kisses her salty lips."

Passerby: Wow. It *is* sparkling. I can't believe the author had to self-publish it before traditional publishers took notice! And that agent, Tanya Pueblo, never even returned the emails he started sending her six months after she received the manuscript!

Other Passerby: What's going on?

Passerby: She's reading a little bit of this novel, Oily, that everyone's been trying to find.

Other Passerby: Ooh, can I listen, too?

User: Well, I wasn't really planning to keep...okay, sure.

Passerby #3: Me too.

User: All right. Why not? Maybe I should stand up. Okay. "In the morning the pale canvas sides of the makeshift tent light up with the sun. Warren awakens and watches Penny breathe for a while, wondering if she feels as serene as she looks. He jumps when the bath salts tin rattles. He digs it out from under the shirt Penny tossed in the corner and pulls off the lid. The probe is closed, all smooth and seamless. For a moment he wonders if it is just a piece of plastic he found and everything else has been a dream. But it speaks: 'Today please drive us to Port Fourchon,' says Jerry's translated voice."

Passerby: Hey guys! She's reading from that book everyone's talking about! Come listen!

Random Passerby: Which book? Oily?

Lifeguard: Would you like to borrow my megaphone?

User: Uh, I guess so. Why not? " 'Right now?' Warren asks.

'Not necessarily,' Jerry's voice replies. 'Today.'

Warren gets up after a while and goes into the house to fetch a glass of organic apple juice for Penny. He brings it out to her, then returns to fry up some organic eggs in an iron skillet and toast some all-natural bread. They eat in the tent, saving out some crumbs and bits of egg for Jerry and Phthsspitty-snapp. An hour later Warren is driving west in the Jetta®, the tin on the passenger seat beside him and Jerry perched on his shoulder."

Lifeguard: You might as well climb up here!

User: But what if—

Lifeguard: Ah, no one's swimming right now. Look at this crowd.

Crowd: Oi-LY! Oi-LY! Oi-LY!

User: Wow. Okay. Thank you everybody. I'm going to keep reading, but I can only read a limited amount, and I cannot accept any form of compensation, monetary or otherwise. Just so you know. Okay. Here goes:

"'I'm not sure how close I'll be able to get you,' Warren says. 'They'll have a security gate, fences. Maybe even razor wire.'

'Razor wire?'

'Oh, um...razor wire is this thick wire with sharp points and edges all along it. Prisons coil it along the tops of tall fences to make it very difficult for anyone to climb over.'

'But the containment dome is not built in a prison,' Jerry says.

'Right, right. And I don't even know if they do have razor wire. They might just have barbed wire, which is similar but not as dangerous. It just has sharp points every foot or so. Or they might just have fences.'

'To keep the laborers from escaping?'

'No, ha ha. To keep random people from coming in and maybe stealing things or wrecking something.'

'I will fly the probe over the fences,' Jerry says.

'But aren't you afraid your enemies will find you?' Warren asks.

'It is a risk I am willing to take for the sake of your species,' Jerry replies. 'The containment dome must fail.'"
Crowd: ROARRRRR! WHISTLE! WHOOP-WHOOP!

X. LIMITATION OF LIABILITY

A. Loss of Profits, Wages, Salary, Tips, and Other Forms of Compensation: The creator of Oily shall not be held liable for any user's financial or other losses, including but not limited to any and all losses incurred as a result of:

1. Distraction: Users understand the possibility that any and/or all portions of the text of Oily may distract them from the earning and/or granting of profits and/or other forms of compensation. Users are advised not to read the text of Oily while participating in lottery drawings, radio contests, bicycle races, televised and/or non-televised game shows, quiz bowls, professional sporting events, manual labor, non-manual labor, operation of vehicles and/or heavy and/or light machinery, paid security details, and/or any other activities and/or situations for which they may receive compensation. Users understand and accept the possibility that they may lose track of time while reading the text of Oily. Skeptical users are invited but not mandated to participate in the following demonstration: note the time, read the passage below, and then guess how many minutes have passed before checking the time again. Start now.

"I thought we had thirty days," Warren says.

"Please remain hidden," Jerry says. Warren hunkers down a little lower in his corner of the tent, pulling the rumpled sheet up over his nose.

"I still think we could've used more practice," Penny says from the opposite corner. "What if they shoot their way in?"

"They can't be certain that we are still within this structure," Jerry says patiently. "That was the purpose of our intermittent signals. More practice would have given them more certainty."

"You're sure you can sew us up if we get blasted?" Warren asks.

Jerry's voice drops to a mechanical whisper. "Hmmm's probe is nearing. Remember that the risks you take are for the sake of your entire species."

Warren shuts up and listens for the approaching probe, taking in the sounds of waves and cawing gulls for a moment before he remembers that the probe is silent. Unless it comes in fast, in which case he might hear a faint whoosh. But he imagines it gliding slowly along the sand, nosing this way and that as it tries to pinpoint the location of Jerry and Phthsspitty-snapp's probe. Jerry finally let them all in on his new plan, explaining the new situation and his hope that Hmmm detected his attack on the leaking riser pipe and launched the probe over the Gulf, then detected Jerry's attack on the containment dome in Port Fourchon and been lured in closer, close enough that their three quick rehearsals in the tent would bring them right in. Warren tries to catch Penny's eye, but he can only see the top of her head as she crouches in the other corner, half under and half behind a big pile of bedding. He tries to concentrate as the minutes tick past, tries to feel heroic, maybe like a pitcher about to take the mound in game seven or a firefighter walking into a flaming house.

Two minutes have passed since you began reading, although you probably experienced the temporal illusion that only one minute passed. Users understand that such an illusion may make them late for appointments, engagements, committee meetings, elementary school Thanksgiving pageants, assignations, town hall meetings, classes, and/or dates.

2. Sleeping: Users accept the possibility that they may experience drowsiness, dozing, napping, nodding off, slumber, and/or sleep while and/or after reading the text of Oily, despite the creator's best efforts to leave out the parts that people tend to skip, and that such snoozing may jeopardize users' earnings. Users are advised to avoid reading Oily while or immediately before directing air traffic, walking tightropes, scaling cliffs, monitoring nuclear power plants, driving freight trucks, guarding valuables, teaching children, operating light and/or heavy equipment, playing shortstop, refereeing children's tee-ball games, and/or any other activities for which they may be remunerated. Any and all losses of remuneration incurred as a result of sleepiness and/or sleep are the sole responsibility of users. Users under the influence of antihistamines, motion-sickness pills, turkey, anti-nausea medications, chamomile tea, sleep aids, warm milk, antidepressants, crème de

menthe and/or any other substance known to induce drowsiness are cautioned against reading Oily during and/or before any activities for which they may be remunerated.

The creator of Oily understands that some users may be unsure of their degree of susceptibility to drowsiness. Such users are invited but not mandated to read the following excerpt, which is among the most stimulating passages within the text of Oily:

"Here it comes," Jerry whispers. Warren holds his breath. He keeps his eyes on the flap that serves as a door to the makeshift tent, but he catches movement out of the corner of his eye. The late-afternoon sun striking the canvas on the left side of the tent gives it a bright glow, and the shadow of Hmmm's probe moves slowly across it, a sharp silhouette. It pauses, then moves around the back end of the tent. Warren knows after a moment that it must be just a foot or two from his head, and he fights back the image of green fire shooting out of the probe, tearing the flimsy canvas behind him and blowing a hole in his skull. The waves and gulls keep up their background commentary, and in the tent nothing moves. He feels a little woozy and realizes he should take a breath. Penny, in the far corner, has the same look on her face—eyes wide, lips tight. He catches her eye and makes a show of sucking air in through O-shaped lips. She gives a micro-nod and inhales. But then the tent flap moves and Hmmm's probe floats in.

As planned, Warren erupts from his corner, flinging bedding aside and brandishing a little shrimp net. He lunges at the hovering acorn and manages to strike its tail end with the wire frame of the net. Warren stumbles to his knees and scrambles to pivot around, not sure where the probe is now.

Once he has turned around, he finds it at eye level, just out of reach and pointed straight at him. He freezes, wincing and wondering again whether Jerry can really treat a hole in the head.

Penny rises up from her corner, reaches out with her shrimp net, and neatly catches the probe from behind, then pins it to the ground. Warren lunges again, yelling a garbled war cry and grabbing the probe with both hands. "Careful!" Penny shouts. "Point it that way! Point it that way!" He rolls over, still screaming like a charging warrior, and holds the probe at arm's length, aiming it at the tent's front door. It buzzes in his hands, and a thick line of faint green light burns through the canvas. It pulses again and sears a clumsy C through the cloth. The probe tugs at his hands, but it is easy to keep it from making any headway. Wow, Warren thinks, and then Penny is behind him, shoving at his shoulders and shouting, "Take it out there!" He struggles to his feet, both hands still gripping the probe, and pushes through the smoldering tent flap. Penny follows him. "The sand! The sand!" she yells, and he remembers to point the probe down. It buzzes and tugs over and over, melting sand and leaving squiggles of bubbly glass. "Just keep holding it," Penny says, not quite yelling now. "It should stop in a minute."

"They're talking," Warren guesses. That was the plan. He and Penny stand there catching their breaths, wondering what Jerry and Hmmm are saying.

If they had the proper equipment, they would hear Jerry saying, "It's over, Hmmm! The monster's got you."

disagreements relate to aesthetics, politics, history, literature, petroleum engineering, environmental science, astronomy, physics, and/or metaphysics. Users understand that the opinions expressed in the text of Oily, whether explicit or implicit, belong solely to the creator of Oily, who is solely responsible for its content but shall not be held liable for any actual or perceived damages, financial or otherwise, resulting from disagreements about said opinions. Users must understand and accept the risk of writing, verbalizing, or otherwise making known their opinions regarding Oily, its content, and/or its implications. For users who do not understand the risks inherent in making their opinions known, the following demonstration is provided.

Supervisor/commanding officer/customer/judge: Reading just relaxes me.

User: Oh, me too. Yeah, I read for an hour or so every night.

Supervisor/commanding officer/customer/judge: Me too. That's why I avoid dry, boring books. I can't read military history in bed. Puts me right to sleep. I love it, but it puts me right to sleep.

User: Right. I'd rather read a fast-paced novel or something.

Supervisor/commanding officer/customer/judge: Sure. Tom Clancy.

User: Right now I'm in the middle of this novel called Oily. It's not bad.

Supervisor/commanding officer/customer/judge: I think I've heard of that.

User: You know—it's the one where aliens come to earth to harvest all of our petroleum.

Supervisor/commanding officer/customer/judge: Right. That's the one.

User: It got me thinking. I wasn't sure how I felt about drilling in the Arctic National Wildlife Refuge, even after Deepwater Horizon. But now I've made up my mind.

Supervisor/commanding officer/customer/judge: Hmmph.

User: It's just not worth taking the risk. We've got to find alternatives.

Supervisor/commanding officer/customer/judge: That's where you're wrong. Speaking of making one's mind up, I've decided to give that promotion to Johnson/transfer you to Greenland/take my business elsewhere/deny your motion.

Although the creator and all future publishers of Oily accept no liability for losses incurred by users as a result of any disagreements or arguments triggered wholly or in part by the content of Oily, users should note that standing up to other users and/or non-users (e.g., by telling off a vindictive, ill-informed supervisor/commanding officer/customer/judge) may be heroic. The creator of Oily is not exactly encouraging such acts of heroism, which are to be undertaken at users' own risk, which users should consider embracing.

XI. ARTISTIC LICENSURE

The creator of Oily hereby declares that he possessed a valid artistic license at the time this TOU went to press. Said license was issued by the International Artistic Licensure Consortium in 1978 and is a lifetime license with no expiration date. Users understand that the creator's IALC license permits him to take liberties with grammatical, social, literary, formal, and/or physical conventions and/or traditions. Users accept their obligation to tolerate such liberties and attempt to understand their aesthetic value and/or purpose. Such liberties include but are not limited to intentional misspellings, sentence fragments, and verb errors; unrealistic dialogue; unlikely personal transformations; subversion and/or flouting of the conventions of narrative; unrealistic and/or impossible feats of strength, quickness, and/or agility; breaches and/or ignorance of the fundamental laws of physics; and manipulation of genre conventions. Users objecting to liberties taken by the creator of Oily have the right to report perceived abuses of artistic license to the International Artistic Licensure Consortium, which will review such complaints on a case-by-case basis and make whatever determination it sees fit. Users wishing to report abuses of artistic licensure should visit http://www.IALC.co.antarctica and click on "Report Abuse."

Users wishing to test their ability to tolerate such liberties are invited to read the following sample passage from the text of Oily:

Makeshift canvas tent. Late afternoon sunshine. The sound of waves, two-foot waves, rolling lazily into the sand. And from within the crooked, sagging tent the sound of voices, two of them tinny and mechanical, two of them just regular. "So then it's settled," Warren says. But that comes later.

Inside the tent! Warren and Penny lie stretched out on their stomachs, propped up on their elbows, facing one another. Between them a rough arena of rumpled canvas. What are they doing? Watching a showdown between two teams of two pill bugs?

"This is an outrage!" one of the pill bugs is saying, its voice emitting from a tiny speaker on its shoulder. And of course you can guess who this pill bug is, that his name starts with an H and ends with three M's. "Your career is over! You can be sure that I will be filing insubordination reports with the Exploratory Board, and I suspect they will contact the attorney general's office immediately."

"So I broke some rules," Jerry says. He takes a step toward Hmmm, jaw set. "The same rules that say we should wipe out an entire species that gets in our way." He gestures upward, toward Penny and Warren, who do their best to look wronged.

"You'd rather let billions of Xxzzrrrvans starve to death?" Hmmm demands.

"Hol' on," Warren sez. "What?"

"Have you taken a good look at this species?" Jerry asks, again waving an arm at Penny and Warren. "They're Xxzzrrrvans, too."

"Preposterous!" says Hmmm. At some point every aristocratic villain must use the word "preposterous."

"Back up," Penny says, matching Warren's puzzled expression.

"Gravy, place this man under arrest," Hmmm says. "And his protégé." Turning back to Jerry, he says, "We're taking you in. Please command these brutes to relinquish both probes."

"Why don't I command these brutes to squash you like a bug?" Jerry snarls. He glances at Warren, who obligingly raises a fist and bares his teeth.

"You wouldn't dare," Hmmm says, due in part to his obligation to use the word "dare" periodically.

"What have I got to lose?" Jerry says.

"Did they say what I think they said?" Warren asks Penny.

"Two things," she says. "But I'm not really sure."

"We've got to find out," he says, and she nods as they return their attention to the little bread-plate arena between them, where Hmmm is shouting about the Exploratory Board's authority and Jerry is shouting about moral authority. "Excuse me," Warren says, but the shouting continues. "Jerry? Hey! We've got questions."

"The Board of course takes such things into account," Hmmm is saying.

"The Board most certainly does not," Jerry begins to say, but a spray of sand knocks him over before he can get the words out. When he picks himself up, he sees the fleshy wall of Warren's hand blocking his view of Hmmm and Gravy.

"Can I say something?" Warren asks. Neither alien answers, and so he speaks. "What do you Xxzzrrrvans do with the oil, with the petroleum?"

"Many things," Hmmm says. "It fuels our vehicles, coats our rooftops, powers illuminators, communication devices, and the like...."

"The same things you do with it," Jerry says, then adds, "And we eat it."

Penny shudders.

"You eat it?" Warren says.

"It's not the only thing we eat," Hmmm says indignantly.

"Although at this point it makes up approximately 57% of a typical Xxzzrrrvan's diet," Phthsspitty-snapp adds quietly.

"You just...drink it? Crude?" Penny says.

"Certainly not!"

Jerry waves Hmmm away. "Mostly tar," he says. "Some paraffin. Various consistencies. Aerated tar, when freeze-dried, forms a comestible similar to your 'toast.' And we've got soft, flavored paraffin that resembles your 'butter.'"

"What I wouldn't give for some bitumen cheese right now," Phthsspitty-snapp says dreamily. "Or an asphalt-burger."

"Did you always eat it?" Penny asks. "I mean, even in primitive times?"

"Of course not," Hmmm says. "The practice arose out of necessity due to food shortages. I believe it began when a chef of the southern continent ran short of lettuce and found that he could approximate the texture by rolling tar into paper-thin sheets."

"Is lettuce extinct on your planet?" she asks.

"By no means. But it is expensive, as are most fruits, vegetables, grains, and products made from the eggs and milk of the Cwortchokchok."

"But nutrition...?"

"Tar is a good source of carbohydrates, although of course both tar and paraffin are high in fat. But they are high-calorie substances, and so small amounts usually suffice," Hmmm says.

"Wow," Penny says.

"Yeah, wow," Warren says. And the six of them blink at one another. "So...what can we do to keep you from wiping out our species?" Warren asks Hmmm.

"Nothing at all," Hmmm declares. "The survival of our own species depends upon what remains of the petroleum reserves you have stolen from us."

"Go ahead and squish him," Jerry tells Warren.

Warren reaches out with his thumb and index finger an inch apart. "I'd rather not," he says. "But if that's what it takes...."

The tiny dots of Hmmm's eyes close. He stands still for a moment, until his knees give way and he kneels involuntarily. "Perhaps...perhaps we can discuss some alternatives," he says.

XII. ACKNOWLEDGMENTS

The creator of Oily has included explicit mention of any and all organizations, individuals, and/or other entities whose financial, social, emotional, and/or physical support was significant during the making of the text of Oily, and the creator of Oily shall instruct any and all future publishers of Oily to likewise include the aforementioned mentions. Accordingly, acknowledgement is extended to all who fall into the following categories:

> A. Supportive Family Members: The creator of Oily wishes to thank his parents, mother-in-law, siblings, siblings-in-law, nieces and nephews, as well as his spouse and children. Forms and degrees of support have varied from family member to family member and include but are not limited to respecting the efforts of the creator of Oily, taking such efforts seriously, inquiring after such efforts, congratulating the creator of Oily upon his individual successes, wishing him well, reading published texts by the creator of Oily, recommending such texts (including the text of Oily) to others, leaving alone the creator of Oily on weekend mornings and even fixing her own waffle and getting herself a drink, refraining from borrowing the computer on which the creator of Oily composed the text of Oily, critiquing early drafts of the text of Oily,

proofreading galleys of the text of Oily, being tactful about Oily, delivering invective against clueless publishers and editors for rejecting Oily and other texts, cursing literary agent Tanya Pueblo for requesting the manuscript of Oily and then not replying for six months and responding not at all to polite emails or even voice mails, assisting in the creation of book trailers, and acting as sounding boards.

In honor of supportive family members, the creator of Oily includes the following passage in the text of Oily:

"How are you feeling, though?" Warren asks Penny on the way to the electronics store an hour inland.

"I'm sure it'll work out," she says, gazing out at a shrimp boat chugging up the bayou.

"No, not about this," he says. "I mean, physically." He wants to tell her she looks better but fears he is wrong. He looks past the clumped hair and camping grime, thinking he sees a faint glow that has been missing for so long.

Penny sticks her lip out thoughtfully, parting the canvas she wrapped around her body before getting in the car. She glances down at herself. "Well," she muses. "Not too bad, really. Kinda better."

Warren nods happily, eyes stinging. "I mean, I wish we could be out in a forest somewhere in the middle of nowhere where the air was really pure instead of here in oil country, and if somehow we could go a whole month without using the car, but I'm glad it's helping."

"I still feel kind of weak, but I haven't had the nausea, and look at my arms." She holds one out, skimming her hand over the fading rashes.

"Woo hoo!" Warren says, turning up the radio, which is playing an old familiar song about the importance of family, immediate and extended, and about how their support allows one to accomplish significant things. "If my parents hadn't given me their old Jetta®, I don't know what we would have done," he says between choruses. "And my brothers and sisters are awesome, as are yours and your parents, not to mention our respective extended families!"

B. Supportive Friends and Acquaintances: The creator of Oily wishes to thank buddies, former classmates, pals, people he used to know, childhood friends, colleagues, fellow writers, non-fellow writers, neighbors, Facebook™ friends, and folks whose names and/or faces he knows for whatever reason. Support from such personages has included but has not been limited to attending readings in which the creator of Oily participated, saying hi to the creator of Oily at the entrance to a nearby grocery store and/or from the passenger seat of a passing vehicle and/or at a festival downtown and/or elsewhere, appreciatively acquiring Oily as a free download and/or reasonably priced print-on-demand book, critiquing drafts of Oily, posting reviews of Oily on Goodreads®, and recommending Oily to their own family members, friends, colleagues, acquaintances, strangers, and/or other persons. In honor of friends and acquaintances, the creator of Oily includes the following passage from the text of Oily:

"Hi, how can I help you find the perfect technology solution today?" says the man in the red shirt.

"Howard?" Warren says.

"Right," the man says. "Oh, hey Warren! What are you doing here?"

"Just kind of browsing," Warren says, cupping his hand and dropping it by his side, hoping the four aliens on his palm won't get jostled too badly. "This is my wife, Penny."

"Hello," Penny says.

"Howard teaches part-time at the college," Warren explains. "Sometimes."

"Yeah, I picked up just one class this semester, so I got the job here to supplement."

"Can you believe this BP® oil spill business?" Warren says. He crosses his arms, still gingerly cupping the aliens, so they'll be sure to hear the conversation he hopes he is about to have.

"Oh man," Howard says, shaking his head. "You heard about the containment dome? It didn't work. I'm starting to realize this is going to just go on and on. The Gulf is ruined."

"Right, right," Warren says. "It makes me want to get rid of my car, just get off the grid altogether."

"We've got to find some alternative before we ruin the whole planet," Howard says. "She's mother earth, and we're not taking care of her health."

"Absolutely," Warren says. This is perfect! he thinks. Friends and acquaintances can be so supportive of one's efforts!

"So are you guys really just browsing?" Howard asks.

"Afraid so. Actually, we're in the middle of a camping trip down at Grand Isle, and we just needed to use a computer for a minute," Warren confesses.

"Not a problem! Browse away. Just find someone in a red shirt if you have a question or whatever."

Howard drifts off, and Warren and Penny stand in front of the biggest touch-screen computer they can find. Warren furtively drops Jerry, Hmmm, Phthsspitty-snapp, and Gravy in front of the keyboard. "This is the device I was telling you about," Warren murmurs. "The communication device that accesses a global network of similar devices, upon which information is stored?"

Jerry's voice comes faintly. "Understood."

"I'll pretend you're talking to me," Penny whispers.

"Good idea," Warren says. "Okay, so look. Are you wearing those translation goggles? If I type 'end oil dependence' into this search engine—which searches for whatever text I want on billions of documents in the network—I get...over eight million results. Or look at this—'end offshore drilling' gets over five million. 'Alternative energy' gets sixteen million. Or ooh, I know. Let's look up wind farms, which are collections of gigantic—even to us—wind turbines that generate electricity for human communities. See the photo?"

Hmmm speaks a little too loudly. "And what fraction of Earth's electricity is produced by wind farms?" he sneers.

"Okay," Warren says. "Good question, good question. Let's see here...probably not very much, but...okay. Two point five percent. I know that's not much, but it's going up all the time. Look at this graph—it's increased almost tenfold in the past ten years."

"Huh. Interesting," Penny says. "What about hydroelectric power?"

"Right, right. Oh, um, you mean electricity produced by water-driven turbines, for example inside of a giant dam spanning a large river? Let's see—ooh! Sixteen percent of the world's electricity!"

"That's very good."

"And you know what? Coal is big. I think most power plants use coal. Wait...Okay, about forty percent of Earth's electricity is produced by coal. You guys don't eat coal, do you?"

"No," Jerry says.

"Look at this," Penny says, putting her finger on the computer screen. "Oil is only used for about five percent of the world's electricity."

"Oh. I thought it was a lot more. See? That's not much."

"And yet your planet consumes billions of oobalings each day," Hmmm says. "How many of your vehicles utilize coal?"

"Fair enough," Warren says. "But soon we'll be able to buy electric vehicles from major manufacturers. A lot of companies have fleet vehicles that run on natural gas. Here's a site on alternative energy. There are tons of these sites. 'It is crucial that we develop clean, renewable energy sources now, before we deplete Earth's supply of petro'—never mind. See, though? Lot of people are working on this."

"And while they are working on it, billions of vehicles on land and sea or in the air burn our petroleum," Hmmm says.

"It's true the alternative energy movement is moving slowly," Jerry concedes. "But, as we discussed, we may be able to accelerate it considerably."

"Right," Warren says, and no one speaks for a grave moment.

Howard drifts past. "You guys still doing all right?"

Warren nods.

"He's so nice," Penny says.

"He does seem quite nice," Jerry says. A nearby television shows images of a dozen young people on a beach, laughing and being handsome/beautiful around a campfire.

"Just having the support of friends, even acquaintances, is so important," Warren muses. "But anyway. Which species?"

"Something cute," Penny suggests. "Penguins or pandas. I mean, I would hate that, but it would get people's attention."

"Yes, but how much has the world changed because cute animals like pandas—which are furry black and white vegetarian quadrupeds—are endangered, meaning that it has been determined that their numbers have declined to a level that raised the possibility of extinction?" Warren asks. "And penguins—as you know, Penny—are flightless aquatic birds native to the south pole of our planet."

"Some," she says. "But maybe not all that much."

"I saw a companion animal," Phthsspitty-snapp says, making rare use of the translator Jerry has outfitted her with. "Is that common?"

"Quite common," Penny says. "OMG, that would cause an uproar. Cats or dogs. Dog owners would probably be the most vocal."

"Yes. Dogs are descended from wild canines. With their exceptional genetic elasticity, we have created dozens of breeds of all shapes, sizes, temperaments. They were domesticated thousands of years ago, and besides serving as companions, they assist ranchers pursuing livestock, guard homes and businesses, retrieve hunters' birds, assist police officers pursuing wrongdoers, and detect the presence of drugs, bombs, and dead people."

"And are these animals of economic importance?" Hmmm asks.

"Well no," Warren says. "They're just—or wait. Actually." He looks at Penny.

"You're right," she says. "Pet food, toys, groomers, accessories. It's a billion-dollar industry."

"But is it reversible?" Warren asks the aliens. "Like what if a few dogs were quarantined or sent into space until it was over? Could they come back and repopulate the planet with dogs?"

"Never," Hmmm says.

"Maybe not dogs," Penny says, and Warren shakes his head.

C. Former Teachers: The creator of Oily thanks all teachers, instructors, professors, teaching assistants, student teachers, mentors, and others whose words and/or actions have been instructive in settings and locations that have included an elementary school, a junior high school, a high school, two universities, and two writers' conferences. Forms and extent of support from such personages has varied and has included but is not limited to instruction in reading, writing, penmanship, and typing; guidance in the interpretation of literature and other works of art; explicit and implicit guidance regarding the planning, composition, revision, and/or editing of specific literary works; and the modeling of attitudes, viewpoints, aesthetics, and/or stances. In honor of former teachers, the creator of Oily has included the following passage:

"And...action," Warren says, clicking the button on the little video camera he bought from Howard. He also bought a cellular modem for the laptop. Jerry sashays into view and turns to face the camera. Warren lowers his head to the sand to squint at the display, making sure that nothing is visible but Jerry and the sky behind him.

"My name is Jerry," Jerry begins. "I am the lead scientist on a Xxzzrrrvan expedition to Earth. We came here to assess the progress of our petroleum-farming endeavors. Our ancestors seeded this planet with life billions of years ago, knowing that their descendants would return to extract the petroleum, which is crucial to our existence. When we meet face-to-face, I can explain this history to you more expansively. For now I want to tell you that your species' use of petroleum is seen by my superiors as theft on a grand scale, theft that threatens our way of life. My superiors have ordered the extermination of your species, as has been done on other planets. I have managed to convince them that your species may be willing and able to give up petroleum and deserves clemency. My superiors have agreed to delay extermination for thirty days, during which time you have the opportunity to surrender your petroleum and secure your survival." Jerry shrugs his front shoulder and shakes his head, then leans more intently toward the lens. "You and your advisors no doubt have questions and concerns. Some will doubt our ability to exterminate your species, just as some will question the evidence that we caused your oil extraction facility to explode. To lend weight to our demands, we have initiated extermination of an important animal species. Within seven days, that species will be extinct. Please reply to the email to which this video is attached with your detailed plan for immediately halting petroleum extraction worldwide." He walks off the plank of driftwood serving as a stage. Warren clicks STOP.

Hmmm, Gravy, Phthsspitty-snapp, Jerry, Penny, and Warren gather in the tent to watch the video. "This is effective," Hmmm says as it ended. "As you said, it is not obvious that we are tiny in relation to your species. But your email must be carefully composed as well."

"I've been working on that," Warren says, tapping the laptop's touchpad. "God, I hope we don't get any sand in this thing. Here it is. I saved it as a draft so all we have to do is attach the video and send it."

Hmmm and the other aliens put on their translation goggles and step closer to the screen, craning their necks to read Warren's email. Hmmm nods. "Quite concise," he says.

"You write very well," Jerry adds.

"Thank you," Warren says. "I have had so many encouraging teachers over the years, who instructed and inspired me in so many ways."

"Teachers are amazing," Penny concurs.

"Especially some of the ones I had at LSU and UNO and at Ben Franklin High School, Acme Junior High, and Lusher Elementary, but also faculty I worked with at the Nebraska Summer Writers' Conference and the Taos Summer Writers' Conference."

"You're going to be a famous writer one day," Penny says.

"Aw, shucks," Warren says, knowing it is true.

D. Employers: The creator of Oily extends gratitude to employers past and present for their support. Forms of support have included but are not limited to pecuniary remuneration; subsidy of travel to conferences; employment benefits; encouragement and/or tolerance of literary ambition; provision of office space, equipment and software; appreciation of occasional publication in minor literary periodicals; and publicity in internal and external newsletters.

The creator of Oily has included the following passage in the text of Oily, in honor of employers past and present.

"I'll be back around four thirty," Warren says.

"It's a shame to use all that gas," Penny says. "Couldn't you just send your students a study guide?"

"I already missed Monday, Tuesday, and Wednesday," he points out.

"I guess we're lucky you have a job where you can just call in and tell them you won't be there. They don't ask for proof or anything."

"Right. Exactly! No one's saying, 'Why are you canceling classes? Are you sick? Bring a doctor's note,' or anything like that."

"Bring us proof that you're too busy saving the human race to teach your classes," Penny says, mock serious.

"They trust me."

"Right. Just like they trust you to go the whole semester making your own decisions about how to teach, how to grade, how to deal with students. You work very independently."

"I'm lucky."

"You are."

Jerry emerges from the propped-up bath salts tin in the corner of the tent, where the probes are parked and he and the other aliens spend most of their time. "Have you received any replies from the White House?" he asks.

"Not yet," Warren says. "They probably get thousands of emails a day, so I think it might take a day or two. Is the toxin ready?"

"It is nearly ready. Hmmm has instructed the crew of the mother ship to begin launch preparations."

"Are you finished with that?" Penny asks, pointing to the raw turkey leg lying on a Styrofoam™ dish beside the bath salts tin. "I want to get rid of it before it starts to smell bad."

"Yes. We have the samples we need."

Penny crawls over to the turkey leg and lifts the dish gingerly. She manages to get through the tent flap without dropping the leg. Warren joins her outside. "I'll throw this out on my way to the car," he says, taking the leg. "You shouldn't be touching mint-green Styrofoam™ anyway."

"I'm glad we didn't do dogs," Penny says.

"Thank God you realized chickens were a bad idea," Warren says. "All those subsistence farmers...."

"I still think rhesus monkeys would have been perfect."

"Yeah, but you can't buy rhesus monkey legs at Piggly Wiggly."

E. Publishers of Previous Texts: Gratitude of considerable amplitude flows also to the editors of periodicals who have published other texts by the creator of Oily, whether those publications have been fiction, nonfiction, and/or poetry. Consequences of such publications have included but not been limited to encouragement, resume building, opportunity, notoriety, and/or progress toward lifelong dreams.

The creator of Oily instructs any and all potential re-publishers of Oily to include the following passage, dedicated to publishers of previous texts:

The tent begins to glow as the sun strikes one side, and Warren shoves his pillow this way and that, turning to face Penny. He studies her sleep-softened face, trying to picture how it will look in ten years, or twenty, then realizing again how her face has changed in the past week or so. Some color has come back, so that it is no longer all one pale, ill hue, and the bags under her eyes have shrunk considerably. He takes a breath to speak but thinks better of it.

He hears the faint click of a probe opening and raises his head to look in the corner. Jerry hurries out from under the bath salts tin, waving his arms. "Tune your device to Cable News Network™," he shouts, then ducks back under the tin.

Penny wakes up as Warren scrambles for the laptop. "What's happening?" she asks blurrily.

"Something on the news," he says, tapping keys. She sits up, finger-combing her hair.

By the time the live feed starts rolling in, the anchor stands in front of an image of a flooding river in Missouri. "We missed it," Warren says.

"No, but look—go here," Penny says, pointing to a link, and after a moment he finds another link: Mystery Ailment Killing Turkeys. As the video loads, the four aliens troop out of their tin shelter and come to stand on the laptop and watch the screen.

"Our next story takes us to Canada, where Brian Jitney reports on the deaths of thousands of gobblers." The story unfolds, accompanied by footage of barnyards and corrals full of collapsed white turkeys. "Authorities speculate that an unknown virus, perhaps food-borne, may have caused the deaths, although nothing will be known for certain until lab results are complete."

"The American president will soon explain the actual cause," Hmmm says.

"No," Warren says glumly. "No, I can see how this is going to go. Why did I even think...? They'll just say it's a virus or something. They'll keep saying that. They'll even come up with a name for it and show images of some microscopic culprit and make up all the fake science that goes with it. They'll track us down and arrest us and kill you guys and shoot down the mother ship. The president is just another politician. Nothing'll change, and the next Xxzzrrrvan expedition will wipe us all out." He falls back and sticks his nose in the crook of his elbow.

"It's only just begun," Penny says. "They're still speculating. As it spreads worldwide, they'll have to explain it. And you know what? If the president ignores our video, we'll put it on YouTube™ and it'll go viral. People will link to it on Facebook™, and they might even start to organize protests or some kind of action campaign. Come on. We can do this." She shakes his arm, and he moves it aside, lifting his head. Penny stares at him, and all four aliens stand on the edge of the laptop giving him serious looks. He sits up.

"You're right," he says. "This is different. Nothing like this has ever happened before." He feels better, her words and their attention having pulled him out of a steep dive. He is like a writer who gets an acceptance letter from a literary journal after a long dry spell, or maybe a writer who meets one-on-one with a New York literary agent and finds that she is quite interested (having read the first chapter), which gives him the energy and confidence to conduct a major revision. He has the courage to continue, which is so important to a writer and to guys who are trying to save the human race from destruction at the hands of aliens.

F. Animals: Some portion of the unlimited store of gratitude flowing from the heart of the creator of Oily is reserved for animals, particularly cats, dogs, birds, rats, squirrels, hamsters, gerbils, lizards, alligators, fish, cows, pigs, crawfish, shrimp, crabs, and oysters. Forms of support have included but are not limited to companionship, entertainment, and sustenance. Special recognition is reserved for certain cats, certain dogs, certain rats, and the alligators of Cane Bayou and Barataria Preserve.

The following passage is included in the text of Oily as a way of recognizing animals:

By the end of the day, the turkey story has climbed several rungs up the news ladder. "Authorities are now saying that millions of turkeys have died in Canada and thousands in the Pacific Northwest," the anchor says. "Several farms have lost every single turkey. The cause of the illness is still unknown, although it appears to be airborne."

"Poor turkeys," Penny sighs.

"Just think if we had done dogs," Warren says. "This would be the biggest story of the year. People would have had mass demonstrations demanding answers."

"The devastation, though. Are you saying we should have done dogs?"

"No, but if turkeys don't work we might have to."

"The funny thing is, every dog on the planet would be willing to die to save its owners."

"You're right. If there was a dog president and you explained the situation, he would be like, 'We'll do it' before you even finished talking."

"And he would tell all the other dogs, and they would all wag their tails."

G. Anyone Forgotten: It is possible that there are personages, institutions, organisms, and/or other entities whom the creator of Oily has not thought of and who nevertheless deserve explicit expressions of gratitude and whose support may have taken various forms, including but not limited to provision of food and/or beverage and/or other material goods, prayer, putting in a good word, admiration, positive vibrations, fondness, inspiration, and/or repair of vehicles and/or appliances. Any future publisher(s), if any, shall not be held liable for any damages, perceived and/or actual, resulting from a lack of gratitude on the part of the creator of Oily.

The following passage is dedicated by the creator of Oily to such personages, institutions, organisms, and/or other entities:

"Have you checked your email lately?" Penny asks, in the middle of a long afternoon.

"I checked it about half an hour ago," Warren says. "Nothing new."

"Check it again."

Warren sighs and opens the laptop. "This thing is almost out of juice," he says. "I'm getting pretty tired of going inside to charge it up. Wait—there's an email from the White House." They exchange a look. "Here we go. Call the aliens!"

Jerry pops out from under the tin. "What is happening?" he asks.

"I have an email from the White House," Warren says. "Come see before I run out of juice."

All four aliens clamber across the bed sheets and climb up onto the laptop. "Okay," Warren says, and moves to click on the email. "HIBERNATING," the laptop announces, the screen going blue. "Damn it!" Warren says. "We'll have to go inside."

"Do I understand correctly that the computer has little power, and that you have no receptacle into which to affix the cord and access the electromagnetic network that powers your illuminators and other devices?" Jerry asks.

"Basically."

"One moment." Jerry confers with Gravy, who nods. "Please show Gravy the end of the computer cord," Jerry says, and Penny digs it out of her bag. The aliens confer again, Gravy tugging at one prong of the plug experimentally. More alien discussion, and then Jerry addresses Warren. "With your knife," he says. "Can you cut the plug off the end of the cord?"

"I could..." Warren says.

"Very well." Without another word he and Gravy hike back toward their corner and disappear under the tin. Phthsspitty-snapp sits on the spacebar while Hmmm paces across the touch pad. After a few minutes Jerry and Gravy reemerge, wrestling a black thing the size and shape of a vitamin across the hills and valleys of the sheet. Penny takes it from them, and they climb back up onto the laptop.

"What is this thing?" she asks.

"A sort of battery," Jerry says, then tells her to get Warren's knife, which she does, but she hesitates before cutting off the plug. "I promise that your computer will still function well," he says.

"Cut it off a few inches higher," Warren says. "If we have to, we can splice it back together."

"That won't be necessary," Jerry says, and Penny saws the cord, holding it against the back of a book in her lap. The aliens guide her through splitting the cord and stripping the insulation off of the wires. Then Gravy gets to work, untwisting and re-twisting the wires, turning the vitamin battery this way and that, until the cord and the battery are one.

"Are you sure about this?" Warren says. "It's a tiny battery."

"It is not exactly a battery," Jerry says. "Not like your batteries. Place it in sunshine."

Warren pushes the end of the cord out the door onto hot sand.

"It works," Penny reports. "Hang on a sec...Here we go. 'Thank you for your recent email to WhiteHouse.gov. You can be sure that your email has been reviewed carefully by White House staff. However, the volume of mail received makes it impossible for staff to respond individually to each message. Your concerns and/or suggestions and/or opinions have been noted. Thank you.'"

H. Not Tanya Pueblo: The creator of Oily wishes to make it clear that literary agent Tanya Pueblo is excluded from any and all acknowledgments of contributors and supporters. Neither the content of her presentation at the writers' conference nor her specific comments to the creator of Oily in private proved to be of any use to the creator of Oily, who has concluded that literary agents merely interfere with and lengthen the complex process of bringing a writer's work to the public, for writers must endure months of impatient speculation after sending to agents work that agents have requested they send, and those agents sometimes neglect to respond at all, despite repeated attempts by writers to contact those agents via email and/or voicemail and/or U.S. Postal Service, and if the coldness of an agent's shoulder has anything to do with a writer running into an agent on an airport shuttle and saying that his next book would be about mental telepathy, which admittedly may have sounded somewhat ridiculous at first blush with no time to really explain the whole idea, then maybe an agent is somewhat unprofessional and should not even continue to be an agent.

XIII. DEDICATION

By clicking "Agree" below, users accept and appreciate the dedication of Oily by the creator of Oily to a single user. Neither the creator nor any future publisher(s) of Oily shall be held liable for any damages, actual or perceived, resulting from dedication of

Oily to another user. All users, including family members, friends, acquaintances, former teachers, employers, publishers of previous texts, animals, and/or anyone forgotten accept that the user to whom Oily is dedicated merits exceptional gratitude as well as love, admiration, and support from the creator of Oily. The decision to dedicate Oily to the spouse of the creator of Oily was made solely by the creator of Oily, and any consequences resulting from that decision are solely the responsibility of the creator of Oily.

As dedicatee, the spouse of the creator of Oily accepts the dedication, whatever her doubts about the text of Oily, even if she currently believes and/or at some point believed that writing a sci-fi novel was not the best use of time and/or energy of the creator of Oily.

By dedicating Oily to his spouse, the creator of Oily acknowledges and even celebrates not only his love for his spouse and her love for him, but also his obligation to her for literary assistance, which includes but is not limited to assistance with proofreading, suggestions for endings, global critiques, encouragement, suggestions of markets, informative facial expressions, solicited and unsolicited laughter, etc. Other users understand, however, that the creator of Oily wrote the entire text of Oily himself.

The influence of the dedicatee varies from chapter to chapter, from passage to passage, and even from sentence to sentence; influence varies from subtle to specific. Even the creator of Oily may have difficulty identifying exact influences on specific passages, such as the part where Warren and Penny are in a panic, striding down the beach, struggling to look casual while at the same time getting away from the tent as quickly as possible, spooked by what they saw on the news, spooked in part because having a hand in the top two news stories can send a sense of vertigo through the human body, but also spooked because of unexpected seriousness. "Not that I thought it was child's play or something," Warren says to Penny in the aforementioned passage.

"He was so grim," Penny says. "So threatening."

"I noticed there has been no discussion of our role in the explosion of the petroleum extraction device or in the failure of the 'containment dome,'" Jerry says from his position on Warren's shoulder. "Do you suppose no one is aware of the damage we inflicted?"

"I'll bet they know," Penny says. "I mean, they wouldn't know where it came from, but they must have seen the damage and recognized that it was mechanical or whatever."

"And so they have not told the newsmen, or have the newsmen not told the viewers?" Jerry asks.

"Or have they told the newsmen not to tell the viewers?" Warren asks.

"Neither the government nor the journalists or Xxzzrrrva would be so insidious," Hmmm scoffs.

"Oh really?" Jerry says.

"All that stuff about bioterrorism and 'We will bring responsible parties to justice, swiftly and surely,' though," Penny says. "I mean, I guess it kind of is bioterrorism, isn't it?"

"I guess they have to give people some kind of answer. With the oil spill, it looks like an accident, so they can act like it is. With the turkeys there's all this clamoring for answers, so they've got to say something," Warren says. He stops beside a limb of driftwood and a tangle of seaweed to turn and look back at the tent. It is hardly visible, a sandy speck on a long stretch of sand. "You sure that guy had binoculars?" he asks Penny.

"Yes, I'm sure. I guess he could have been a birdwatcher...?"

"That's exactly what they want us to think," he says. Warren and Penny eye each other until the moment crumbles and they both laugh. "Did I really just say that?"

The night is hot and Warren sleeps without sleeping, in part because he is sweating and in part because thoughts and half-dreams of marked and unmarked law enforcement vehicles harass him all night. "What's the latest?" he says aloud after the sun begins to shine in earnest, waking Penny, because he knows the aliens have been watching CNN™ all night in their probes. Jerry emerges a few minutes later and climbs up onto the laptop to tell Warren and Penny that turkeys in Europe and Asia have begun to die, a "top hat" device is being prepared as the next attempt at capping the well, and oil has begun to foul the barrier islands. Warren rises to a crouch and moves toward the tent flap when Jerry adds, "And your president will tour the coast today." On his way to the bathroom, Warren thinks about their next move, but even the notion of sabotaging the top hat can't override his urge to run and hide. Back in the tent, Penny is awake with the computer on her lap. "Read these," she says, handing him the laptop before crawling out of the tent and heading to the restroom. It is the YouTube™ page for the video of Jerry that they sent to the president, which Warren posted the night before. He tries to decide whether 200 views and 14 comments are encouraging numbers, but he imagined it being a worldwide sensation by now. "I think you're right, Human242," someone named SnakeBit has commented. "Just another marketing ploy. They're trying to create a buzz for some new movie or maybe even a TV show." Aside from a couple of comments along the lines of "OMG! Is this for real?" it is mostly speculation about CGI, with Julia45284 dismissing the whole thing as "just some guy in a cheesy jumpsuit turning his body sideways."

Users understand that the spouse to whom Oily is dedicated may have pointed out a typo, such as "turnkey" for "turkey," stated that she was not sure where this conversation took place, suggested that the dialogue end sooner, and/or pointed out other errors and/or made other suggestions regarding this passage and/or made broader suggestions which affected this passage more indirectly. Users further understand that such actions do not make the spouse of the creator of Oily a co-author, but do make her a worthy dedicatee, as do the love and support she provides to the creator of Oily.

XIV. WARNINGS

A. Combustion: Users are cautioned against exposing print-on-demand or traditionally published copies of Oily to open flame, oil-soaked rags, sun-struck magnifying glasses, active compost piles, engine compartments, curling irons, and all other heat sources or potential heat sources. By clicking "Agree" below, users indicate comprehension of the fact that printed copies of Oily are flammable. Flammable portions of Oily include the passage in which Warren lies on his back in the tent, one arm covering his eyes, sharing a jar of organic pine nuts with Penny as she sits cross-legged, brooding. He worries over the knotted circumstances, wanting to keep Penny free of petro-allergens, wanting to sabotage the top hat, wanting to disappear and never get arrested as a bio-terrorist, and wanting to save humankind from the Xxzzrrrvans. Hundreds of waves wash up against the beach as he turns the problem this way and that. "Jerry," he says at last, to the little alien in the corner. "What was it you said about the president?" He sits up and looks at Penny. "Go to whitehouse.gov," he says, and she digs out the laptop.

Let's see," she says, not having to be told to find the president's schedule. Jerry and Hmmm climb up onto the laptop. "The president will be in Venice in about an hour."

"We'll never make it," Warren groans. "We're doomed."

Users are advised to take care not to rub the above passage rapidly against adjacent passages in such a manner as to create heat sufficient to ignite paper.

B. Eye Irritant: Users who choose to read Oily are hereby advised and cautioned that extended use of Oily may cause symptoms of eye irritation, including but not limited to redness, itching, bleariness, rheum, ache, strain, and tearing. Users are advised to discontinue use of the text of Oily whenever any symptoms of eye irritation occur and to consult a physician before resuming use of the text of Oily, even if users have read as far as the requisite dark hour before the dawn, with Warren despondent, fending off all of Penny's attempts to console him, which include assurances that the YouTube™ video will go viral, that thousands will march upon Washington, that oil companies will surrender to Xxzzrrrvans. He just shakes his head, at one point lying face down and groaning miserably. She tries another tack, saying they'll kill dogs next, and then people will listen—or wait, better yet, they'll kill mosquitos or cockroaches, show themselves to be well-intentioned, even heroic. "There's no time," he moans. "Grassroots movements don't just spring up overnight. People can't just read our minds and pop up out of nowhere."

"Maybe we can get an extension," Penny says. "Sixty days, or ninety." She looks hopefully at Jerry and Phthsspittysnapp sitting nearby.

"Not possible," says a voice, and Hmmm climbs up from the tin in the corner. "The mother ship staff has already prepared the toxin and has irrevocable orders to launch it in 25 Earth days."

Warren sits up. "But where did you get a tissue sample?" he asks. "Oh. While we were sleeping. I should squish you." Hmmm loses considerable dignity as he scrambles down off of the tin, but Penny gingerly snatches him up. "Get that bottle," Warren says, but she's already picking up the soy nuts jar, and she pops Hmmm in and puts the lid on tight.

Users experiencing eye irritation at such a point in the narrative must discontinue use, despite any sense of suspense or impatience, even if numerous friends, acquaintances, relatives, and/or colleagues have finished reading Oily and users have read reviews of Oily in national publications and/or seen its creator on television and/or heard that a film starring Jake Gyllenhall and that girl from Alice is in the works, all of which may seem unlikely to anyone familiar with the fate of 99.9% of self-published novels, but which is still possible, considering the presence of the creator of Oily in social media and the fact that the creator of Oily's perception of the excellence of Oily is not entirely naïve, as might be the case with a raw neophyte, given the creator of Oily's training and experience and tendency to make frequent reality checks, although writers always believe their work is better than it actually is and the trick is to learn how to make the gap between perceived and actual quality as narrow as possible. The creator of Oily realizes that it may take years for the novel to accrue the critical mass of readers to the point where a traditional publisher sits up and takes notice, eventually launching a publicity campaign that causes users experiencing eye irritation to wish to carry on reading despite their discomfort, which they must not do and for which the creator and publisher(s) of Oily (if any) shall not be held liable.

C. At-Home Imitation: Users, non-users, semi-users, and all essential and nonessential personnel must UNDER NO CIRCUMSTANCES attempt any stunt, non-stunt, trick, move, maneuver, deed, ploy, number, scheme, gambit, ruse, artifice, tactic, or non-tactic demonstrated within the text of Oily. Characters and non-characters within the text of Oily are fictional (see Article IV), and just as professional drivers on closed courses can control sports cars more safely than amateur drivers on public roadways, fictional characters can more easily carry out actions that would be dangerous, difficult, and/or impossible for actual persons in actual situations, particularly in science fiction and/or fantasy and/or magically realist narratives. By clicking "Agree" below, users promise not to attempt to:

1. Sabotage or interfere with oil exploration, extraction, and transport devices and facilities;

2. Visit oil spill sites in unauthorized water craft;

3. Capture, ambush, or touch alien spacecraft;

4. Fail to report genuine, verifiable encounters with aliens and/or alien spacecraft to the proper authorities and/or media outlets;

5. Drink, ingest, and/or imbibe petroleum and/or petroleum extracts and/or products, except those approved by the FDA and/or USDA;

6. Commit acts of bioterrorism;

7. Pitch tents in unauthorized locations and/or places;

8. Concoct a last-ditch attempt to save mankind which involves sitting with one's spouse in a tent with a laptop, watching a live video feed from an alien probe as it flies at a high rate of speed over a stretch of Gulf made gray by an overcast sky, a blob ahead resolving into a ship, growing a little bigger, and then disappearing, a spindly drilling rig easing by on the right, white flecks of smaller boats coming and going, getting more numerous not long before strips of green color the horizon. Users understand that this portion of the TOU refers to the scene in which Warren tells Penny, "They're pretty close now." The land extends in spider fingers into dark Gulf water, and then the water gets browner and the fingers thicken before the earthy river slides into view and the probe stops over a ribbon of pavement lined with buildings.

The dangerous scene which users must UNDER NO CIRCUMSTANCES imitate continues with Jerry's voice crackling out of the laptop's tinny speakers. "We have reached Venice," he says.

"Okay, look for a commotion. Look for a line of vehicles, most of them black. There might be police cars with flashing blue lights at each end of the line...? Unless they've already gotten there, in which case look for the same kind of vehicles in a parking lot, maybe not in a line."

"I see a collection of buildings to the southwest," Jerry says. "Surrounded by cars of various colors. Many of them are black."

"That's it. I see it. Now be careful. There are lots of police officers and soldiers and secret service agents all over the place." As Warren and Penny watch, the probe drops slowly over a low, sprawling building. Men are on top of the building, here and there at the edges, cradling rifles, but none of them are looking up, and the probe glides along ten feet above their heads. To one side a small crowd surrounds an open tent.

"I can hear him," Jerry says. Warren turns up the laptop volume, and a faint voice comes through. He and Penny lean forward slightly, listening, but there are no surprises—nothing about extraterrestrials, quitting oil cold turkey, or saving the human race from extinction. As the speech ends, Warren leans forward, heart pounding. "Now watch carefully," he whispers to Jerry. For a few minutes there are murmured questions and amplified answers, and then suddenly the crowd shifts and parts, armed men trot here and there, and a tight knot of people emerges from the tent. "You see him?" Warren whispers. There's no answer, but the probe speeds up a little and dips down above the knot of people, then flies up and away. "Did he jump?" Warren asks. "Phthsspitty-snapp? Did it work?"

"One moment," Phthsspitty-snapp says. The knot, the parking lot, the building recede as the probe rises higher, but then it stops and the image zooms in on the man in gray at the center of the knot. Just as he is hustled into a large black SUV, Phthsspitty-snapp manages to get a tight shot of the tops of his shoulders and head, and then he's gone and the door closes.

"Did you see him?" Warren asks. "Did he make it?"

"Analyzing the image," she says. "I think...yes. Look at this."

The live video of the SUV easing forward goes blank. After a moment, Warren and Penny see closer view of the president ducking into the vehicle with a dark speck on one shoulder. "Is that him?" Warren asks, and instead of replying Phthsspitty-snapp dials up the zoom tenfold, magnifying the speck until it becomes Jerry, riding the president with two fists full of jacket and a big grin on his face. Warren turns to Penny and they execute a sloppy combination of high fives and fist bumps. "Now we wait," Penny says.

XV. SPOILER ALERTS

Attentive users who have carefully read this Terms of Use Agreement perhaps realize that it is possible to glean the principal shape and many of the details of the narrative within the text of Oily from this Terms of Use Agreement. Users who do not wish to discover the principal shape and/or details of the narrative are advised to avoid reading this agreement, particularly the present article, which includes material which gives away the ending of Oily. For the purposes of this agreement, "ending" refers to that part of the text of Oily which begins inside of the richly appointed dark interior of the black SUV, where Jerry tries to find a stable place on the president's shoulder. "What did Putin say about the alien video?" the president asks a man to his left.

"He still hasn't responded," the man says with a shrug.

The ending of Oily continues with Jerry clambering from the president's shoulder to the top of the seatback and positioning himself where he can duck under the headrest if anyone takes a swipe at him. "Mr. President?" he calls cautiously.

"What was that?" the president asks. "Did someone's earphone fall out?"

"Mr. President, my name is Jerry. I am the alien you saw in the video. I am right behind you." Jerry braces himself, standing just one step beyond the shelter of the headrest.

The president turns, his famous face looming just inches from Jerry's, and he raises a hand swiftly. Jerry dives under the headrest. "No, it's all right," the president says. Jerry lifts his head and sees that the president has cupped his hand at the top of the seat. Jerry stands up and steps onto the hand. "Gentlemen," the president says to the men around him, who have yet to notice what is happening. "This is an historic moment." Jerry does his best to stand up straight as all eyes turn his way, even as a man in a dark suit draws a gun and holds it ready. "Put that away," the president scoffs.

"We have been waiting to hear from you," Jerry ventures.

"Yes, I understand. I wish I could have replied immediately. Your video underwent extensive analysis, which took some time. My advisors and I, and some select cabinet members, have had extensive discussions regarding the best course of action to take regarding your message. And of course the oil spill and the turkey crisis have demanded attention."

"But have you chosen a course of action?" Jerry asks. "There's not much time."

"You have to understand that reactions among members of my administration have varied widely. My military leaders are calling for a search-and-destroy response, despite the convincing evidence of your ability to wipe out an entire species. Others have called for complete cooperation, while still others believe negotiating to be the wisest option. Just this morning I began contacting leaders of select foreign nations—"

"Mr. President," Jerry says. "We have a saying on Xxzzrrrva: 'If you are freezing to death, burn the rule book.' My government considers my refusal to exterminate humans immediately an act of treason. I'm not sure how much longer I can hold them off."

The president pauses, lips tight. "We have begun discussions of a cooperation plan, which involves a twenty-year period of adjustment to allow us to find alternative energy sources while phasing out oil production...."

"Sir," Jerry says. "If I were the leader of my planet, I would grant you a twenty-year period of adjustment. But I am just a scientist and an astronaut, and I have thrown away my career to give your people a chance to surrender. My planet depends on petroleum much more than yours, for all of our fuel and building materials and much of our food. Our planet is enormous and has a population of several trillion. The government is willing to go to war to protect its petroleum resources."

The president studies Jerry for a moment, then gazes around the ring of faces watching dumbfounded. He looks out the window at the drizzly landscape speeding by. "I'll go down in history as the one who surrendered," he says softly.

"Or as the one who saved the human race."

"Probably both. Companies will crumble. Millions will be out of work. Entire nations will fall apart. Commerce will grind to a halt. You're throwing us back to the dark ages."

"Perhaps. But my human friend expressed great amazement at a bit of Xxzzrrrvan technology that may be of great use here." The president is looking sad, and so Jerry speaks quickly. "It is a form of solar power developed centuries ago by our scientists. It has limited applications on Xxzzrrrva, which is enveloped in thick clouds and somewhat more distant from our sun. We use it to power small mathematical calculators and outdoor lighting that never lasts very long. But we have found that here on your sunny planet it produces surprising amounts of energy. My earthling friend calls it hypersolar."

"Interesting," the president concedes.

"I believe your planet has the necessary minerals and technology to produce these hyper-solar cells."

"Sounds promising," the president says.

Jerry thinks for a moment. "A hyper-solar cell the size of a vitamin provided plentiful power for my friend's laptop," he says.

The president sits up a bit. "For how long?"

"All day."

"What size hyper-solar cell would be required to power a vehicle, say this vehicle?"

"I have no way of calculating with any precision, but I would guess that a cell the size of a piece of toast would suffice."

"To power this exact vehicle, without significant weight reductions or loss of power?"

"I believe so."

More scenery-studying and face-gazing. "Gentlemen," the president says, gazing more purposefully now at the faces surrounding him. "A change of plans." He addresses Jerry. "This evening I will make an historic announcement," he says.

And so the very ending of Oily begins with Warren at the last minute thinking to set Hmmm's soy-nut jar nearby so that he can see, too. Gravy sits comfortably on the space bar while Warren and Penny sit cross-legged, shoulder-to-shoulder. Finally the chatty anchors interrupt themselves, and the president blinks calmly on the screen, seated at his desk. "My fellow Americans," he begins. Warren feels tingly and lightheaded, and he can tell by the look they exchange that Penny does too. They lean forward.

Jerry's probe noses through the tent flap just as the president says good night. Only the glow of the screen lights the tent now, but Warren sees the long acorn silhouette glide in for a landing beside the bath salts tin. The tingly vertigo is gone, replaced by a dull ache in his chest.

"That's it?" Penny asks, as the anchors and pundits take over. "Maybe there's a p.s."

"No, that's it," Warren says.

Jerry and Phthsspitty-snapp come hiking across the bed sheets. "We had some difficulties in taking our leave," he calls. "Have we missed the announcement?"

"You didn't miss much," Warren says, flopping back onto the ground. He hears tiny, distant gibberish—Hmmm shouting in Xxzzrrrvan from his jar.

Jerry and Phthsspitty-snapp join Gravy on the space bar. "Please explain," Jerry says.

Warren just groans, so Penny speaks up. "He announced a six-month moratorium on deep-water drilling," she says.

"That's all?"

"That's all. And now oil industry experts are squawking that it'll cripple the economy."

Warren moves the soy-nut jar into the corner of the tent, hoping it will be out of earshot. "What's he saying?" he asks.

"That I had no authority to represent Xxzzrrrva in negotiations with your president. And that I have betrayed my entire planet, for which I will suffer for the rest of my life."

"We, meanwhile, have failed our planet. And so our species is doomed." Warren turns his back and puts a pillow over his head. "Good night."

He refuses to move for a long time. The aliens, embarrassed, retire to their probes. Penny clicks at the computer for a while, then shoves it away and lies on her side next to Warren, one hand on his hip. He feels her wanting him to turn her way and open his eyes, but he resists, pretending not to know what she is saying. Finally he sighs and rearranges himself to face her. She smiles slightly, and of course he knows what she means. Their eyes meet, and she gives him the look that signifies *I feel so much better now, almost back to normal, thanks to you. See?* He tells her how glad he is, but one eyebrow insists on pointing out that it doesn't matter much, now that the human race is doomed. *Don't give up,* her eyes say. *It's not too late.* He glances away, and she knows he is thinking, *Yes it is. We've got a deadly addiction to oil. Look what it's done to us and to the planet.*

The firming of her lips says, *But we've got to keep trying.* She glances toward the glowing computer. He says *Huh?* with his eyes. She does it again, and he squints thoughtfully. *Make another video?* he asks, and she gives a microscopic nod. *Tell people the truth, the whole story? Show them the aliens and the probes? Announce that the human race is about to be exterminated?*

She gives him a kiss that means *It's worth a shot,* and he expels a sigh that means *I don't think it'll do any good.* "Come on," she says, and they sit up.

The Terms of Use Agreement is in no way intended to give away the entire ending of Oily. Users are advised to find out from the actual text of Oily itself that Penny keeps the camera and a rechargeable spotlight pointed at Warren as he moves around inside the tent, saying, "All right, so some people thought our first video was fake and/or a commercial for a sci-fi movie. But it wasn't. Look in here. See that little guy? His name is Hmmm and he's some kind of big shot on his planet, like a vice president or something. He's the one ordering the extermination of the human race, because his ancestors set up our planet millions of years ago to produce petroleum, and now we've stolen and wasted most of it and they need us out of the way so they can salvage what's left. Look over here. This is Jerry and his intern, Phthsspitty-snapp. Jerry is a hero, because he has been trying to save the human race, and he threw away his whole career to do so. He's got a little translator. Say something, Jerry. Okay. See how they're just like us, only sideways? And a lot smaller, of course. Shine the light over here. These are their spaceships or whatever. See? Gravy, are you in there? There's one more alien, a pilot named Gravy. Gravy, are you in there? Fly the probe around the tent a bit if you are. No? Okay. Jerry, by the way, spoke to the president today, and the president said he would take action, but all he did was announce the moratorium. Should've known. He's just another politician, and it takes politicians years to get things done. But we don't have years. We've got about three weeks, and then we'll start dying the way the turkeys are dying now. That's right, the aliens killed the turkeys. It was supposed to demonstrate to the president what they were capable of. I feel sorry for the turkeys and the turkey farmers and all. The aliens also caused the oil spill. Jerry did that to try to convince Hmmm that we didn't have the technology for deep ocean drilling yet so maybe we shouldn't be exterminated, but it kind of backfired. Let's go out here. Just a sec. Oof. So we're camping on the beach here on Grand Isle because my wife is allergic to petroleum products. Those are the lights of the fishing pier down there. And now they're saying the oil is about to wash ashore right here and ruin this whole place. So I guess that's it. Turn it off. Turn off the camera."

"Wait," Penny says. "Tell people what they should do."

"What they should do? Well, it's the president who needs to—and the leaders of other nations. And the oil companies. What can regular people do? Maybe if there was some kind of mass action, like if everybody got out and demanded that something be done. Show the politicians, even the alien politicians like that little guy in the jar, that we'd rather live without oil than die. But it has to be right away, and it has to be big, and what are the chances of that? Okay? How's that? Can you turn off the camera now?"

Users are advised not to read the following section of this TOU, which reveals the essential elements of the very *very* end of Oily, containing a lengthy excerpt from the part where Warren and Penny sit cross-legged on their bedding, the laptop glowing before them. A little shadow moves out of the corner, and Penny reaches out a hand to save Jerry the trouble of hiking over the many fabric hills and valleys between him and the computer. She sets him down on the caps-lock key. "This is the video we made," she explains, as Warren fiddles with the laptop. "We're setting up a separate Facebook™ account for both videos, also putting them on MySpace™ and a few other sites."

"So many hoops to jump through," Warren grouses, clicking I AGREE. "If we actually read these TOU's we'd never get anywhere."

"Translation failure," Jerry says. "Tea o' use?"

"Terms of Use. Whenever a person registers to use a service, which is available on the global computer network, like maybe a site which allows people to upload videos to the global network, the person has to first agree to the terms of use, which are presented in a lengthy document written by people who...specialize in presenting arguments before judges? And so the document explains exactly what service the site offers and exactly how it is supposed to be used and exactly what the provider's obligations are and what the user's obligations are and what the provider will not do and what the user is not supposed to do and what happens if they do what they are not supposed to do. Or you have to agree to the terms of use when you install a computer program or register a product, so they can have proof that they told you not to use the service or program or product to commit crimes and that they told you they could kick you off of the service and explained exactly what they do and do not guarantee. So you see? Now I'm clicking 'Agree' so I can sign up for MySpace™, even though I have not read the TOU because no one has the time to read these things. Look at it—it must be thirty pages long! I just have to assume that by clicking 'Agree' I'm not promising them half of my income or the soul of my firstborn child, so I guess I trust these corporations to a certain extent. But even non-corporate organizations have these agreements now, like Craigslist, which is this public-service kind of site where people can post little ads when they have something to sell, and I can understand why they have them, because if someone uses Craigslist to commit a crime—which people do, actually, sometimes—then Craigslist has to be able to show a judge the record of that person's agreeing to the terms of use, which says that Craigslist is not to be used to commit crimes, so the victims of the crime can't sue Craigslist, but of course they can still sue the person who committed the crime. TOU's are just another kind of agreement that holds society together, in a way. I mean, explicit agreements have been part of our evolution as a civilization. You could even say the Code of Hammurabi—which was one of the very earliest recorded set of laws, from, I don't know, ten or fifteen thousand Earth-years ago—was basically a TOU. Or what about the Ten Commandments? I don't know if you have religion on your planet, but there's a sort of holy legend that says that God gave a fellow named Moses two flat pieces of stone on which He had written ten rules that people had to follow—things like 'Thou shalt not kill,' 'Thou shalt not steal.' If people broke those terms of use, they would not get to go to heaven, which is the nice place where people go when they die, supposedly. Then you've got the Magna Charta, the US Constitution, and really any law or ordinance. Even when people get married—do you have marriage? It's when two people in love officially become lifelong partners. Penny and I are married. Didn't we talk about this before? Anyway, the marriage ceremony includes a sort of oral TOU where the two people promise to take care of each other for the rest of their lives, and of course the government requires that the people also sign a document, which is not exactly a detailed TOU, but it makes their promises legally binding. So I guess any time people enter into a relationship, whether it's commercial, personal, or legal, there has to be some kind of explicit agreement about the nature and limits of the relationship. Although when people have children they don't have to make any explicit agreement about parenting—well, except that they sign their names to the birth certificate, which gives them certain legal obligations, including adherence to explicit laws. Plus some religions have ceremonies that parents and newborn babies participate in. But it seems like TOU's could be simpler, and I wish they were—they could just say, 'By clicking here you agree to abide by the laws governing the use of web-based email' or whatever, and the laws themselves could be lengthy documents about what's guaranteed and what's not and the penalties for using it to commit a crime and so on, but no one would have to read the laws themselves unless there was some kind of problem. Here's another one—I've got to click 'I have read and accept the terms of use' before I can open up the video-editing software that came with the camera. I don't know how I feel about terms of use. On the one hand, they're annoying and big corporations use them to protect themselves from litigation. Before you know it, we'll have to sign a TOU just to go to a movie or read a novel! On the other hand, they are mostly common sense and they protect small businesses and organizations. They're also kind of like direct democracy—maybe it's better to be offered the explicit regulations regarding the use of these things up front, instead of just agreeing to follow laws that we haven't seen. And laws take so long to put in place. Governments move about as fast as glaciers, which is maybe why there are so many TOU's these days, since the internet is fairly new. It takes too long for governments to hammer out the details, and so people just do it themselves, at least until government can catch up. Maybe we should have more of them. Maybe if the oil companies had signed terms of use a hundred years ago, the planet would not be so unhealthy, and neither would Penny." Warren stops talking. He looks at Penny, studying her face in the whitish light of the computer. "Penny," he says slowly. "I just realized something."

"I know," she says. "I know you did. I'll finish this." She turns the laptop and sets her fingers on the keys. "You go on in and get started."

He gives her a kiss, stands up, and leaves the tent. "Where is Warren going?" Jerry asks.

"To work on his masterpiece," she says.

Soon Penny closes the laptop, arranges a pile of bedding to her liking, and falls asleep. Jerry hikes back to the probe and joins Phthsspitty-snapp watching Star Wars™ on the central display. One window of the rented camp remains illuminated, and behind it Warren sits at the kitchen table with a mug of strong coffee and a ballpoint pen.

The sun has floated up above the horizon by the time he emerges from the camp and slogs through the sand to the tent, a roll of floral shelf paper under one arm. He swipes at the tent flap and falls in beside Penny, turns this way and that for a moment, then lies still, smiles at her, and closes his eyes. Penny studies him for a few minutes before stretching and sinking back into sleep. Close to noon she gets up and walks over to the camp, returning an hour later with damp hair and a platter of toast and eggs.

"It flowed right out of me," Warren tells her while they eat. Jerry, Gravy, and Phthsspitty-snapp sit on the lid of Hmm's jar, munching on crumbs the size of their fists.

"How long is it?" Penny asks.

Warren leans back and fetches the shelf paper from one corner. He unrolls it, revealing neat lines of handwriting on the back side. "Six or seven feet, I guess."

"I'll start typing it up after we eat," Penny says.

"May I see?" Jerry asks, and he peers at it through translation goggles while Warren holds it close. "Our translators have yet to master your handwriting," he says. "I will wait until it is typed."

"Here," Warren says, and holds the shelf paper rather like a king's messenger holds the announcement of a ball for all eligible maidens in a kingdom. "'Before proceeding, all parties must agree to the terms of use detailed in this document, written by and on behalf of the undersigned occupants and inhabitants of Earth. By clicking AGREE below, all governmental entities of Xxzzrrrva and Earth and their representatives accept the principles enumerated below. One: Surrender of petroleum...' Well, it would take a long time to read this whole thing to you, but basically it says that we have to give Xxzzrrrva our oil, but that Xxzzrrrva has to give us five years to find alternatives, although Xxzzrrrva can extract oil from reserves we haven't tapped yet with no limitations during those five years and that we will taper off our oil use over those five years.

And in return, Xxzzrrrva will not exterminate, kill, or harm anyone or damage the planet. Even if someone asks Xxzzrrrvans to wipe out species they think are detrimental, like mosquitoes, Xxzzrrrvans will not comply, because nature has a delicate balance and everything. They'll also help us engineer hyper-solar devices and such so that maybe we can make a seamless transition. Then there's this long part about how no government on Earth or Xxzzrrrva can request changes or delays or anything, that any laws relating to stuff in the TOU will have to be written and enacted after the TOU is signed because there's no time to wait. I figured Hmm wouldn't go for it otherwise. What else…It also says that no one will get paid for the oil, but that if Xxzzrrrva needs help from us they'll pay for the help, or if they use existing facilities they'll pay for their use, but the costs will be the same as they would be if earthlings used the facilities. Of course, then there's the problem of how Xxzzrrrva gets Earth-money, but I realized that we would be able to buy oil from Xxzzrrrva during the five-year weaning period. One of the later articles is about surrendering all supplies of gasoline, diesel, kerosene, and other fuels and/or liquid derivatives of petroleum by the end of the five years, if Xxzzrrrva wants them. It also says that Earth shall keep its supply of plastics. I figured Xxzzrrrva could not use it, though maybe you can, but it's going to be hard for us to wean off of plastics and so I figured we would need to recycle what we've got until we can figure out the alternatives. And then there's the question of reparations for all of the petroleum we've already used, and I said that Earth would not pay Xxzzrrrva for that because adjusting to life without oil is going to be expensive enough, plus it appears that Xxzzrrrva had some role—maybe accidental—in our development as a species on this planet. There's more, but it's mostly boring details. Basically I tried to come up with something that both sides could agree to."

"No one else could have written this," Penny says. "It's brilliant."

Warren smiles dreamily. "I'm sleepy," he says.

And so he dozes all afternoon while Penny types, working her way slowly down the scroll. She gives him the numbers on the new video along toward dinner time, when he sits up to take a sip of water. "Three thousand, four hundred and seventy-two views on YouTube™," she says. "Six-hundred and forty-five shares on Facebook™." A couple of hours later, as the sun sinks down, she stops typing just long enough to provide another update. "Almost twelve thousand views, about four thousand shares." After dark he gets up and goes into the camp to round up some tortilla chips, salsa, and cheese, and when he brings them to her and convinces her to stop typing for a few minutes, views are up to 84,310 and shares are up to 23,774. The typing goes a little faster once he starts dictating the TOU to her from the scroll, and they work that way deep into the night, finishing in the wee hours. "It's over thirty-four thousand words," she says. "And we're up to two million, nine hundred and twelve YouTube™ views; one-point-four million Facebook™ shares. I'd say it's officially gone viral. Now we just post the TOU as a petition, get a billion signatures by Friday, and present it to Hmmm and the United Nations on Monday...."

Penny and Warren lie back to front while Jerry stands on the laptop with his translation goggles on. She feels Warren wondering if they can handle all that is about to happen and gives his hand a reassuring squeeze. She tightens her grip again, harder this time, and he knows she is telling him to steel himself for it, to keep his head on straight. *I will*, he says, with a deep sniff of her hair.

Only Oily itself contains the text of the very very *very* end of Oily, which begins with Warren opening his eyes at first light to find Penny watching him. "Today it really starts," he says, and she nods.

They sleep further while the rest of the world drinks coffee, eats breakfast, checks Facebook™, watches a two-minute video, and shares it with its friends, many of whom have already seen it, until a sound begins intruding into Warren's dreams. He hears a murmur, deeper than the whisper of the Gulf against the sand. Someone laughs loudly in the distance. Faint rumbling. When he awakes, he sees Penny studying the sound, looking here and there at the blank canvas overhead. She sits up, and as he follows suit she is standing. As he struggles to his feet, she parts the canvas door and slips through. By the time he gets outside and sees the endless crowd of people on the beach with their signs and tents and hats and kites and guitars, Penny is already running toward them, plump and rosy, ponytail flashing in the sun.

| I AGREE | EXIT |

Acknowledgments

I have several kind people to thank: Susan Woodward and Jalan Woodward for support and feedback during the writing and revising of Oily; Troy Rosamond for feedback and encouragement; Franciscan University of Baton Rouge for valuing my creative work; Nate Ragolia of Spaceboy Books for enthusiasm and wisdom.

About the Author

Angus Woodward was born to southerners in a northern state and moved to Louisiana in 1987. His previous books are the short-story collection *Down at the End of the River* and the novel *Americanisation: Lessons in American Culture and Language.* The Oxford American hailed *Americanisation* as "a hilariously crafted postmodern novel." Angus has two wonderful daughters, and he teaches writing at Franciscan University in Baton Rouge.

About the Publishing Team

Nate Ragolia was labeled as "weird" early in elementary school, and it stuck. He's a lifelong lover of science fiction, and a nerd/geek. In 2015 his first book, *There You Feel Free,* was published by 1888's Black Hill Press. He's also the author of *The Retroactivist*, published by Spaceboy Books. He founded and edits BONED, an online literary magazine, has created webcomics, and writes whenever he's not playing video games or petting dogs.

TJ Stambaugh received several commendations for his bravery as a battalion commander in the Meme Wars. TJ retired to Catonsville, MD, where he paints and enjoys movies you have to read. He's the founder and El Presidente of MoleHole Radio.

Shaunn Grulkowski has been compared to Warren Ellis and Phillip K. Dick and was once described as what a baby conceived by Kurt Vonnegut and Margaret Atwood would turn out to be. He's at least the fifth best Slavic-Latino-American sci-fi writer in the Baltimore metro area. He's the author of *Retcontinuum,* and the editor of *A Stalled Ox* and *The Goldfish,* all for 1888/Black Hill Press.